Dream Snatcher

By **Popcorn Taylor**

Illustrated by Robert Schoolcraft

ROBERT,
I THANK YOU FOR
THE GREAT ILLUSTRATIONS!

Popcorn Taylor

Tasty Titles, a Technics Publications brand

www.TastyTitles.com

Published by:
Technics Publications, LLC
Basking Ridge, NJ 07920 USA
info@TechnicsPub.com

Edited by Tracy Seybold
Cover design and illustrations by Robert Schoolcraft

ISBN, print ed.   9781634621137
ISBN, Kindle ed.   9781634621144
ISBN, ePub ed.   9781634621151
ISBN, audio ed.   9781634621168

First Printing 2016

Library of Congress Control Number: 2016939953

To Jenn, my constant obsession

Contents

Show-N-Tell 1

Hole-In-One 27

Beam Me Up...........................53

My Best ASSet 85

Lust or Love? 129

New Hope..............................159

Hello, Goodbye 191

Second Chance?......................233

End of the Rainbow 255

Caught 285

Controller 307

Show-N-Tell

"I told you it works."

"What works?" I ask Siyo and do not get a response. The loud repetitive clicking sound is a constant reminder that we are going higher and higher. Why couldn't we just ride the Ferris wheel or carousal? And why did we choose this first car? I turn to Siyo and he is smiling back at me, his hands already straight up in the air, getting ready for the roller coaster drop of a lifetime.

"I hear the first drop is wicked. Over 500 feet! Can you believe that?" Siyo lowers one of his hands to rub my shoulder. "Aren't you having fun?"

"It is taking forever to reach the top of this coaster's first hill, and I feel anxious knowing what's ahead. Look around. We are higher than any other ride in the park. The cars in the parking lot look like Matchbox cars."

"What?" Siyo asks. "Matching cars? All of the cars on this ride look the same."

"Matchbox cars," I say louder, over the clicking sounds of the chain gears that are still bringing us higher into the clouds.

"Oh," he replies and again both hands are in the air, anticipating the stomach-dropping exhilaration.

It is a gorgeous day, not a cloud in the sky. I glance behind me, and the car behind us is empty. In surprise, I look beyond the second car and see that all of the cars are empty! "Why are we the only ones riding?"

"Oh, didn't I tell you? It might have skipped my mind. They had major maintenance problems with this ride over the last few days. Cars kept becoming undone after the second drop, and several amusement park guests lost their lives. This is the first day they have reopened the ride. In fact, I heard this is the first time the ride is running since it reopened. Isn't that the best? Kind of adds another level of excitement, doesn't it?"

Siyo must have noticed the color drain from my face or the look of complete shock and fear. "Don't worry, Jenn, you have me with you. I will take care of you." He rubs the back of my neck.

Okay, so there is a good chance we are going to die on this ride. "Sorry, Mr. and Mrs. Bradley," I can hear a park official tell my parents when the house phone is answered. "Jenn's car launched after the second drop and landed several miles away. She is kaput, gone, extinguished." There will be silence on the phone as my parents digest this news. The official continues, "We at the park feel sorry about your loss, as we know Jenn was an only child, so guess what? We are giving each of you season passes!"

"But she would have graduated from high school in less than four months," I could hear my mom sobbing.

My warped sense of humor tries to distract me from my impending doom as I hear the park official respond, "That's too bad. Know what I am going to do? I am going to throw in a lifetime supply of funnel cake!"

"Can you also include churros?" I hear my dad ask.

The park employee is about to respond when the whole conversation evaporates as I realize we are reaching the summit. I look around, and we are the highest point in New Jersey, maybe even in the world.

"Ready?" Siyo asks, still smiling, his hands straight up in the air.

"Do I have a choice? This is going to be the end," I say, imagining our gruesome deaths and holding on to the bars so tightly that my nails dig into my skin.

"Yes, I am your friend," Siyo replies, still smiling.

"That's not what I said." But before I can continue, my stomach drops as we plunge over the peak and rush straight down over a hundred miles an hour. I have been on roller coasters before and even have waited extra time in line to secure the front car, but never have I been down such a grueling drop. We keep falling and falling, and I can see where the tracks reach the bottom before rising for the second drop. I am not even breathing as we approach the bottom at warp speed. I feel like I am going to blank out. I glance to my right to make sure Siyo is not panicking, too, but he is still smiling. In fact, he still has his hands straight up in the air! What a daredevil!

We arrive at the base of the second hill and I breathe for a moment, knowing that the first drop is over. But now the second drop. The one where cars have been thrown from the ride. I close my eyes as we approach the second peak.

"Open your eyes," Siyo says. "You are going to want to see this." He puts his hand on my knee. "Come on, please. I promise you'll be fine. Trust me."

Siyo is one of the most confident students in school. It is amazing he is still so confident when we are probably going to die on this ride. I open my eyes and look at him instead of the speeding tracks underneath. His hair is still neat after the first drop — my hair is probably a mess. Having his long black hair pulled back in a ponytail has always helped him keep his neat appearance. His dark skin and distinctive Native American features, along with being one of the taller kids in school, have always attracted the attention of giggling girls in school hallways.

"That's it, Jenn. Enjoy." Siyo keeps one hand on my knee, squeezing slightly, and the other hand stretches up again as the second drop begins.

I find myself screaming the whole way down drop number two. At least I am breathing. Breathing and screaming. My screams mix with Siyo's laughter. Luckily, it is a shorter drop than the first and very quickly the drop ends, and we are propelled up for the third and final drop. The car is racing up too fast though, I feel it. We are not going to be able to stay on the tracks. We are going to die.

"See, what did I tell you?" Siyo says with confidence.

The car zooms full throttle up the third hill and as we reach its peak, I hear something underneath us break with a sickening snap as we keep going up and up, above the tracks.

Siyo interrupts my screams. "Keep your eyes open, please."

I comply. Now that we are going to die, I might as well enjoy the scenery from this height as we continue to ascend. We continue to go higher, much higher than the entire roller coaster ride. I look down and see the first drop of the massive roller coaster, which seems so small from this height. I know that within seconds we are going to start plunging. What is strange is that we are the only car in the air. What happened to the rest of the coaster cars? I am about to ask this when we start descending.

We are going down, but slowly instead of the deathly plunge that I anticipated. I look up and notice a bright blue parachute above our car.

"Hey, is this part of the ride?" I ask in a hoarse after-screaming voice, still in shock but realizing we may not die after all.

Siyo takes his hand off my knee and puts his arm around me. "See, I told you. All part of this adventure we call life. Enjoy the trip down. We are going to be fine."

I look all around. I never realized the bright colors that canvas the park – the crystal clear blue water where the dolphins perform, the bright green trees speckled everywhere, the vibrant yellow and white stripes of the bumper car tent, and the candy apple red roof of the carousel ride.

"Feel like cotton candy? I can steer our car slightly so we can land right near the concession stand. What do you think?"

I nod my head, still in a state of euphoric disbelief. Siyo leans to one side, and the car moves slightly as we continue to slowly descend. Siyo starts moving his hand from around my shoulders slowly down my back.

I hear an ambulance siren in the distance. The sound is getting louder and louder. I turn to Siyo and he is not smiling anymore. I am about to ask him why he is not happy, but the noise is getting too loud to carry on a conversation.

I woke up. My alarm sounded for another few seconds before I found the off button. 6:55 a.m. on Wednesday. I awoke with such a feeling of exhilaration. Once as a kid, I dreamed that I jumped off a cliff and descended slowly into a swimming pool filled with whipped cream. I had the same rush in this dream and woke up with the same strong sense of control and power. I felt like I could tackle anything today.

Still in bed, I grabbed my phone and texted Siyo.

Me: You up, Siyo?

I got dressed while waiting to hear back. Jeans and a simple button-down shirt, my *high school uniform*. I never invested valuable time selecting the right skimpy outfit for each day of the week, and then additional morning minutes applying makeup and styling hair, like a lot of the other seniors in my high school class. Somewhere between thirteen and sixteen, many of my friends went from wearing comfort outfits to *check me out* outfits, even to our classes. Our school has a policy that skirt length cannot go above the knees, but it has never been enforced, probably because the principal and many of the teachers are men. I never went the *eighteen but look twenty-five* route myself. Whatever I grabbed first out of the dresser I would wear.

I liked boys, and I have not been totally oblivious to their conversations at lunch and how easily they can become distracted when a girl walks by. My jeans were tight-fitting, and I made sure the two top buttons were open on my shirt. I kept one unbuttoned for my parents, and then unbuttoned the second one when I got to school for the boys.

My phone vibrated.

Siyo: Here.

Me: I will never doubt you again.
            That dream snatcher worked.

Siyo: Yeah, I told you.

Me: That snatcher is worth its
               weight in gold. It gave us an
               awesome dream.

Siyo: Hey, I created the dream. The
               snatcher just made sure we
               were both in it together.
               Remember,   Controller   and
               Dreamer? Credit where it is
               due. :L)

Me: lol, okay, Mr. Controller,
               how   about   another   dream
               tonight?

Several minutes pass.

Siyo   Maybe. Let's talk after
               social studies. I'm bringing
               the dream snatcher in for
               show-n-tell :L).

Me: Okay, but keep me out of the
               discussion. K?

Siyo: Of course. CUL8R.

Me: Chow.

The Band-Aid on my finger half hung on, so I
pulled it off the rest of the way. I examined the
paper-cut-looking red line in my skin, a small price
to pay for a magnificent dream. We were currently
studying Native American history in social studies,

and Siyo naturally excelled. Show-and-tell appealed to elementary school kids, but Siyo had brought some of his Native American artifacts into our high school history class this week that had us all mesmerized. He explained even though New Jersey is so built up now, at one point many Indian tribes lived here and occasionally artifacts surface that even surprise history buffs.

Yesterday, Siyo brought an ancient Indian arrowhead to class. He found it while walking on the Seaside beach after a storm. A local historian believed it to be over 10,000 years old.

Today, he is going to bring in that dream snatcher. I can't wait to hear him explain it to the class. Siyo and I have never talked before, but the arrowhead impressed me, so after class I went over to his desk to ask him more about it. He told me he had something even more impressive called a dream snatcher. His house is on the way home for me and when he asked if I wanted to see it, I agreed.

We talked the whole way back to his house about the dream snatcher. I don't remember everything he said, but I do remember the part about controller and dreamer. The controller can enter dreams of the dreamer or completely create new dreams and pull the dreamer in. When the controller pricks the skin of the dreamer with one of the sharp points from the dream snatcher, it allows the controller to control a dream. Siyo orchestrated the entire amusement park dream last night.

I put on a new Band-Aid and emerged from my bedroom to the kitchen, where my parents greeted me with morning hugs, and I deeply inhaled the welcoming smell of coffee brewing. I took a seat at the kitchen table.

"Any interesting stories at the pharmacy yesterday?" I asked my dad. My dad is a pharmacist at one of the last few independent pharmacies in the state. He still worked over fifty hours a week, and most of this time he spent on his feet. Some evenings, my mom and I brought over dinner for him, and he would eat quickly and then return back to work. I learned the value of hard work firsthand by watching my dad at the store.

My dad thought for a moment and then let out a short laugh. "We had a customer come in yesterday with a prescription for Viagra. The prescription looked like someone changed the one in ten to a five. He even used a different colored ink! I called the doctor to double check and sure enough, the customer tried to get fifty tablets instead of ten. He must have been over eighty years old. Can you believe that?"

I giggled. "You can't blame him for trying. Actually he deserves some credit for having an active sex life at that age. Impressive!"

My mom walked over. "You would not believe how many people have an active sex life way into their eighties. Every week, I hear gossip about some of the residents that would rival a daytime soap opera. Who's hooking up with whom? Who just broke up? Who's the cute new man in room 5A that still has all of his teeth? On and on." My mom worked at an assisted living place as a nurse, and she, like my dad, put in long hours and worked hard.

"Did you cut yourself?" my mom asked, noticing the Band-Aid on my finger. My mom has noticed every cut I have ever had as long as I could remember.

"Just a paper cut."

"Your school and our house have heating systems which take moisture out of the air, drying our skin and making us more prone to cuts." My mom shook her head. "Make sure you put some hydrogen peroxide on that next time you change the Band-Aid."

"Okay, Mom." I poured myself a bowl of cereal.

"Would you like some orange juice?" my mom asked.

I nodded, with my mouth full of food.

We chatted some more, and then I glanced at the clock above the kitchen sink.

"Gotta go," I said and jumped up from the table. I placed my bowl and cup in the sink, put on my coat, and grabbed my book bag by the door. "Love you, Mom and Dad."

"Have a nice day," my mom said.

"See you at the pharmacy tonight. It's another late night for me," my dad said.

We lived a little over a mile from school, and I walked at a swift pace to keep warm in this crisp March morning air. I felt excited to talk with Siyo. I had never shared a dream with anybody before. I wondered if he noticed the same things I did in the dream, or maybe he picked up things that slipped by me.

The third period buzzer rang and I made my way to social studies. I saw Siyo gently holding the dream snatcher when I entered the classroom.

"Hey, controller," I said and nudged him a little in his side.

"Hi, Jenn." He blushed. Siyo looked so cute when he blushed. "Did you have fun?"

"Even more than fun. Exhilarating!" A few girls walked by and snickered. What were they thinking? I began to approach them to point out their minds are in the gutter, when the buzzer rang announcing the start of class. We all took our seats.

After thirty minutes of lecture, the teacher said, "Instead of starting the next chapter on the Sioux Indians now, let's discuss another Native American artifact from Siyo's collection." Desks and chairs scraped against the floor as students moved closer to the front to see Siyo's latest treasure. We looked forward to this part of class.

Siyo stood up in front of the class and held up an eight-pointed silver star. Bound to four of the points were a dragon, an eye, linked male and female symbols, and an eagle. "This is a dream snatcher," he said proudly.

"Don't you mean a dream catcher?" the teacher corrected him.

"A dream catcher is a simple hoop usually made from a plant such as willow. Netting is added around the hoop to filter out bad dreams. I don't know if it works though. I think it is more of a way to sell crafts at Indian markets to gullible tourists." The light laughter that followed made Siyo smile and exude confidence.

The teacher nodded.

"A dream snatcher is different. I made up this name. It must have been called something different in the old days. This one is probably over 200 years old." Siyo carefully held it higher for the whole class to see. "My grandfather gave it to me, and he told me it belonged to his grandfather, a well-respected medicine man in the village. This dream snatcher allows the owner to control the dreams of another. If a little boy or girl in the tribe got up at night with nightmares, for example, the owner of the dream snatcher could intervene and help the child better cope with their dreams. My grandfather told me the snatcher can be used in one of two ways – either the owner can enter someone else's dream as just another person in that dreamer's dream, such as with this nightmare example, or the owner can construct an entire dream and make the dreamer just another person in the dream."

Several of the students started glancing at each other, obviously not believing that the snatcher works. I, too, considered myself a non-believer until last night's dream.

The teacher asked for an example of the owner constructing an entire dream.

Siyo thought for a moment. *Please do not mention last night's dream!* Thankfully he didn't. "My grandfather told me how he created a dream that eventually led to him marrying my grandmother. My grandmother, considered the most beautiful woman in the tribe, had been promised in marriage to a powerful warrior. My grandfather told me he created a dream of what their life would be like together, and that convinced her to break up with this warrior and marry him instead."

Several of the girls gave romantic sighs.

"Are both your grandparents still alive today and happily married?" one of the starry-eyed girls who sighed asked.

Siyo looked at the ground, and then responded as even-toned as possible. "My grandmother killed herself right after their tenth wedding anniversary. My grandfather spent the rest of his life heartbroken, and gave me this dream snatcher for my fifteenth birthday."

An uncomfortable silence filled the classroom and several of the students around me looked down to their desks or hands. My mouth opened slightly in shock. The teacher broke the silence. "If you don't mind me asking, Siyo, if this dream snatcher created such beautiful dreams for your grandparents, why did your grandmother take her own life?"

Siyo raised his head and looked at me when he responded. "She began to realize, I think, at least this is according to my grandfather, how beautiful the dreams were and how ordinary and average her real life seemed, and became depressed. The more amazing and romantic the dreams my grandfather created for them were, the more depressed she became. My grandfather, I think, would have never thought she would take her own life though."

Another girl, to change the gloomy subject asked, "So can you enter anybody's dreams with one of these, such as a celebrity or rock star?"

Siyo's expression changed from gloom to grin and a soft laugh escaped his throat. We all joined in with our laughter erasing most of the gloom from the prior conversation. I liked Siyo's laugh. "This is going to sound strange, but you need to draw blood from the dreamer."

"That sounds violent," the girl said.

Siyo didn't acknowledge her comment but instead continued to explain. "You need to prick the dreamer's skin with any one of these four exposed points. I'll call the owner of the snatcher the controller. The controller needs to mark the dreamer." He tapped his finger gently on one of the points, the one that had what looked like fresh-dried blood. I squirmed slightly in my chair, realizing that point punctured my skin to create last night's dream. One of the same points that Siyo's grandfather used on Siyo's grandmother, made my little "paper cut". I felt queasy and moved a little in my chair.

A football player in the room asked, "If we can prick another team's quarterback with the snatcher, can we tackle him in his dreams?"

Several boys howled with laughter and the football player received high fives from nearby teammates.

"You have to be careful with a snatcher," Siyo warned. "I shared a disaster that can come from good dreams. You can imagine the impact of bad dreams. My grandfather told me never to use the dream snatcher unless provoked."

I wanted to ask him what his grandfather meant by "provoked," but before I could, another football player asked Siyo, "Can you score with girls in their dreams?"

The teacher faked a look of disdain while trying to hold in a smile, and Siyo started to answer when the buzzer signaled the end of the period.

I approached Siyo as he gently put the dream snatcher in his book bag. "I wonder if the guys who came up with *Nightmare on Elm Street* knew about this dream snatcher."

He locked eyes with me. "That's just the movies. This is real."

"I know," I whispered back.

As we were both packing up our books for the next class, I asked, "Well, can we?" I didn't want to be explicit in asking for another dream, in case someone overheard.

"I don't know, Jenn." His eyes moved from my eyes down to the floor. "I wanted to make sure you heard what happened to my grandmother. Dreams are dreams, but this is reality."

Siyo collected his thoughts. "I think I like you, Jenn. You are so smart and super pretty." This time, I was the one blushing. I knew because my face felt hot. "I would like to get to know you more, not just in dreams but also in real life."

"Are you asking me out on a date?" I asked, unsure what he wanted.

"If I asked you out on a date, would you say yes?"

"If I said yes if you asked me out on a date, where would you take me?" I asked back and laughed softly at his cautious approach. "Just ask me out."

"Will you come out with me Saturday night?" Siyo asked confidently.

"No, sorry, I already have plans for Saturday," I replied, waiting a few moments for Siyo's look of being crushed to spread across his whole face. I gave him a light jab in his ribs. "Just kidding, Siyo."

His smile returned. "Would you like to do a round of miniature golf followed by Blizzards at Dairy Queen?"

"Yes, sounds fun, but I will pay for my own round of mini golf. Whoever loses pays for Blizzards." Then I added, "Maybe we can plan our next dream together?"

"Maybe," Siyo said cautiously.

Pasta with Red Hots

I always feel aroused after eating chili peppers. A bit of Googling and I learned why. Chili peppers make our bodies release endorphins, which is that same great feeling we get after an intense workout.

These red hots also make us sweat. Sweat, at least up to a point, can be a great aphrodisiac. Also, after eating a couple of peppers, our heart rate increases, pumping blood to all parts of our bodies, and getting us in the mood.

This recipe is easy to make and as a bonus the pasta will give the extra carbs to provide you energy when going miles with that special someone.

Directions:

1. Prepare one pound of your favorite pasta. When the pasta is firm to your liking, add one pound of fresh spinach (or a frozen bag of spinach) to the same boiling water.

2. Heat five tablespoons of olive oil, two chopped garlic cloves, and one seeded and diced chili pepper in a pan. After several minutes, add a dash of red pepper flakes, and salt and pepper to taste.

3. Drain the pasta and spinach and toss with the oil mixture. Add grated cheese if you like (parmesan is my favorite).

Hole-In-One

I told my parents about my plans for Saturday night.

"Where did you meet Siyo?" my dad asked, botching his name completely.

"His name is See-yoh," I corrected my dad. "I started talking with him in social studies, and since then we have become friends. We are taking social studies and Spanish together this term. He asked me out, and I like what we are going to do, mini-golf and ice cream. You can meet him if you like. He is picking me up at five."

My dad nodded.

"I think you'll like him." From *Siyo the friend* to potentially *Siyo the boyfriend*. I have good intuition, and a feeling inside blinked red that this date may not be such a good idea. I didn't know Siyo that well, and even calling him a friend when I described him to my dad sounded like a stretch.

Siyo arrived thirty minutes late. My dad wanted to meet him but had to leave for work. My mom met him though, and I could tell she liked him.

Mini-golf usually gets busy after dinner on Saturday, so we arrived just before the crowds and the empty course gave us time to take each hole seriously. I showed Siyo my competitive nature, even on this first date.

If I didn't choke on the lighthouse hole, I would have kept my six point lead. "Crap. This is the first time ever my ball has hit the lighthouse instead of traveling right through. This club must be slightly bent." I raised the club and studied the shaft to see if it bowed.

Siyo chuckled. The lighthouse hole reduced my lead to four points.

I still maintained a comfortable lead as we rounded the fifth hole, when he asked, "Let's make this game more interesting. How about for every hole-in-one I get, I get to ask you a Truth or Dare question?"

"Do you think this will give you the incentive to beat me? Not likely, I am still four points up, and I can tell you are starting to get tired. Besides, my ace-in-the-hole is the Ferris wheel, which is the next hole. By then I'll be so far ahead of you, you'll get lost in my dust."

"Then you shouldn't be afraid to take me up on this."

"What do I get if I get a hole-in-one?" I asked him.

Siyo took something shiny out of his jacket pocket. The dream snatcher caught some of the light from the tall lamps around us. "I'll give you a dream."

"What about all of your talk about how reality doesn't stack up against dreams, and it is a slippery slope to suicide by using the snatcher?"

Siyo considered this. "I think we can take our chances. As long as our reality is meaningful, I don't think it would make us depressed to share some special dreams."

What he said made sense to me. "Then it's a deal." I stretched my arm out to his, he shook it and we both laughed at the formality. "Remember, we shook on it," I said.

"Yes, that's true. That counts as holding hands, too." He grinned. "You can go first at the Ferris wheel, your ace-in-the-hole, if I can quote you directly." Siyo signaled with his arm in a gentlemanly "you first" gesture, and I put my yellow ball down, and took a deep breath and lightly swung. It went cleanly under the Ferris wheel, but I swung too hard and the ball bounced against the wood railroad tie border, rebounding a few inches and stopping about two feet from the hole.

"Not too bad." Siyo placed his blue ball down and, with a smooth stroke, scored a hole-in-one.

"You rat!" I held the edge of my club at him like a sword. "Where did that come from?"

"Like you said, I just needed an incentive, that's all."

I felt Siyo's eyes on me as I got the ball in on the second shot, reducing my lead to three.

We both picked up our balls, and we were standing facing each other, just a few inches away.

"Truth or dare?" Siyo asked.

"Dare" I replied without much thought, still sulking that I lost that hole. I again mumbled that something must be wrong with my club.

"I dare you to kiss me."

I dropped my club. "Come again?"

"You heard me. I dare you to kiss me."

"That's not fair. Dares are challenges like I dare you to hold your breath for two minutes or make a farting sound with your armpit. You can't dare kisses! Kisses have to happen because sparks fly. You know, romantic music in the background, sharing an umbrella in the rain – like that. It can't be forced."

"A deal's a deal. Kiss me." Siyo did not relent, and he made an exaggerated pucker with his lips.

His silly expression made me laugh. "Fine." I crossed my arms and walked up to him and went to kiss him on his cheek. When my lips were almost touching, he turned quickly and kissed me square on the lips. I backed off quickly, surprised he pecked me on the lips. "Hey, you bamboozled me. I planned to kiss you on the cheek."

"All part of the spoils of war. You just don't like to be beaten in mini-golf. I'll let you go first on the next hole."

"Don't forget who's still ahead, mister. And yes, I do like to win." I focused hard on the next hole. A small bridge crossed a tiny brook, and if you didn't sail the ball across the bridge, the ball would most likely wind up in the water, incurring a three-point penalty.

"Come on, be the ball, be the ball," I whispered.

"I think that is from *Karate Kid*," Siyo interrupted my deep concentration.

"Be the ball." I swung perfectly, and my ball sailed across the bridge and landed right in the hole.

"Yes!" I screamed and jumped up and down to rub it in. "In your face!"

"Nice shot." Siyo gave me a high five.

"You are a pretty good sport for someone losing."

"Hey, I didn't even go yet." Siyo went and his ball also crossed the bridge on the first shot, but it took three to finally get it in, keeping me in first place by five points.

After we picked up our balls, Siyo said, "You get your dream."

The next few holes were uneventful, but Siyo slowly caught up. He would win one, I would win one, but no hole-in-ones.

Siyo got his second hole-in-one on the eleventh hole. "Truth or dare?" he asked me with a big smile on his face.

"Truth." I remembered his sneakiness with the kiss.

"Okay. Share with me a fantasy."

"Come again?" I asked.

"Tell me one of your fantasies. I want it to be revealing, and you can't hold anything back.

Something maybe you think about when you...when you touch yourself. Something nasty."

My face flushed. "Yuck! I don't touch myself, mister." I jabbed him slightly in his ribs with the handle of my golf club. I sometimes did have romantic thoughts, I guess like most people. Should I share my fantasy with Siyo? I didn't know him well yet. I have never ever bailed out on a game of Truth or Dare, however. "If anything comes to mind, I will share it with you over ice cream."

"Fair enough," he said, and we continued to finish the game.

On the seventeenth hole, Siyo got his third hole-in-one. I requested a dare.

"Kiss me on the lips," he said.

"You've done that one already."

"You aimed for my cheek on that last dare. Now aim for my lips." He licked his lips.

With Siyo now ahead of me, losing occupied my thoughts more than a little peck on the lips. I moved in toward his lips for the kiss. As soon as my lips touched his, he grabbed me close and gave me a large open-mouthed kiss. He pushed his tongue into my mouth and found my tongue. I had French-kissed once before and it grossed me out. This time, it still grossed me out. But it also aroused something deep inside me below my belly button.

The kiss lasted for the better part of a minute and when he released me, my self-conscious hoped nobody had seen us kissing. Then I reminded myself how few people were playing at this early hour. The germaphobe in me hoped he had nothing contagious. Finally, the romantic in me hoped he would kiss me like that again. I didn't want the romantic in me to show this soon on our first date.

"Cheater!" I said, catching my breath slightly and jabbing him in the ribs.

"That wasn't cheating. You kissed me on the lips, fulfilling the dare."

"You didn't dare me to French-kiss you. I would have said no way," I defended myself.

"Did you like it?" Siyo asked.

"That's not the point. And it wasn't bad."

"No," Siyo said and licked his lips, "It wasn't bad."

We finished our round of mini-golf. He beat me by two points.

At Dairy Queen, I reluctantly treated for ice cream as part of our deal. I devoured the Salted Caramel Blizzard and he the Peanut Butter Cookie Dough Blizzard. We sat outside on a picnic bench and talked some more over ice cream, and I let him try a spoonful of mine. After all, we had already shared saliva during that French kiss.

After some conversations on school gossip, Siyo asked "So what is your fantasy?"

"First tell me about yourself. I do have a fantasy, but it is personal and I barely know you. I will let you in on it once I get to better know you."

"What would you like to know?" Siyo asked.

"What do you want to do when you graduate? What is your greatest fear? What is your favorite color? That sort of stuff."

"Okay. My dad is a general contractor. Does a good business on home renovations. I have helped him every summer, and I am thinking for at least the first year after high school, I would like to work with him. A father and son team. I am already handy with…"

"What about college?" I interrupted.

"Not for me, at least at this point in my life. I do okay at school, but I like to work with my hands. My dad didn't go to college, and he does well. I see that for me, too. Before I share my greatest fear, what are you afraid of?"

I thought for a minute. "This is going to sound weird, but I don't like biking by myself. I had a bad experience about two years ago."

"What happened?"

"As I rode my bike to a friend's house for her sixteen birthday party, a car slowed down alongside me and the driver reached his arm out and slapped my backside!

I lost control of the bike and fell over. Luckily I didn't get hurt beyond a few scraps. I just felt angry and humiliated. But when I ride, I always feel that something like that will happen again. I get paranoid and keep looking over my shoulder."

"Why would someone do that?" Siyo asked. I liked that he seemed angry.

"I will never know for sure, but after dusting my scraped knees off, I heard the driver say *buen culo*. Do you know what that means?"

"We didn't learn that phrase in Spanish, but I do know what it means. Nice ass."

"Yes, that pervert almost got me hurt."

"He definitely sounds like a loser, but he made a correct observation – you do have a nice ass."

"Gee, thanks," I replied and turned my gaze down to my Blizzard instead of at Siyo. Siyo just dropped a few notches in my book.

After a few moments of silence, Siyo announced, "Now for my greatest fear...you."

"Come again?"

"You scare me, Jenn. You are the prettiest girl in school. You are probably one of the smartest, too. I am afraid…I am afraid I like you more than you like me."

My mouth opened but nothing came out. I knew I blushed. I finished the mouthful of Blizzard and kissed him. He grabbed me tightly again, and his tongue found my tongue again. I could taste some of his peanut butter cookie dough.

"Do you want to hear my fantasy?" I asked after this long kiss.

"I'm all ears."

"Promise you won't laugh."

"Promise."

"Ghosts."

Siyo gave a confused look. I elaborated, "I have a thing for ghosts."

"Okay," Siyo said slowly.

"I think about having sex with a ghost. Okay, I said it. I have been thinking about this since I watched Patrick Swayze in *Ghost*. I want to be taken advantage of by a ghost. I know that sounds weird." I looked down at my Blizzard, realizing I'd never told anyone about this fantasy. My blunt delivery could have been more subtle in how I shared this secret with Siyo.

"No, not at all. In fact, I liked that movie, too. I never thought about sleeping with Patrick Swayze though."

Siyo ended the silence that followed by blurting out "Red!"

"Come again?"

"My favorite color. You asked about that, too."

After finishing our Blizzards, we kissed some more while sitting on the picnic bench.

Siyo glanced at his watch. "Got to get you back home, Jenn. Oh, I almost forgot." He removed the dream snatcher from his pocket along with a Band-Aid. "Let me have that same finger. I don't want to create a new cut. Your parents may get suspicious."

I removed the Band-Aid on my finger and stretched my arm to him. I turned away while he pricked me with the same point he did before. It hurt to have that cut reopened. It felt like a paper cut that got sliced with another piece of paper. I didn't turn back around until Siyo secured the new bandage back around my finger.

"Do you sanitize those points with rubbing alcohol?" I asked. This question my mom the nurse would have asked, but she would have asked it before he cut the skin.

"You're the only one I've used this on. Not to worry."

My heart believed him, my brain knew better.

He dropped me off right before nine, which pleased my mom.

"Who won at mini golf?" my mom asked.

"Your daughter destroyed me," Siyo lied.

"Well, you know Jenn can be pretty competitive," my mom said.

"I know," Siyo agreed. "I asked her for advice on how to play, and she said nothing, completely tongue-tied." He let out a laugh and my mom smiled, but he looked at me when he mentioned my tongue. Very clever with words. I blushed slightly, as he continued to chit chat a few more minutes.

"Seems like a nice boy," my mom said after he left. She would rethink her opinion, if she knew this *nice boy* had his tongue in her daughter's mouth more than once on this very first date.

Being so tired, I decided not to take a shower, and instead I got dressed in my pajamas, brushed my teeth, and went to bed. Besides, the quicker I get to sleep the quicker I see what Siyo planned for me tonight.

I turn on the shower first and then get undressed, giving the water a few moments to get hot and fill the bathroom with steam. I enter the shower and the water feels so good on my body.

I pour some conditioner in my hands and massage it in my hair. Some gets on my forehead, and I close my eyes to avoid the sting of conditioner. I give the conditioner some time to sit in my hair as I scrub myself with soap.

I am rubbing the soap up and down my calves when it slips out of my hand and falls on the shower floor. Crap. I can't open my eyes yet so I bend over, feeling with my hands on the tile. It does not seem to be there. Strange.

Then I feel a touch. A hand against my back. I jump up and slip on the tile. Before I hit the porcelain shower floor, hands catch me from under my arms, and I am brought up to standing again. "Who the hell are you? What are you doing?" I cry, quickly scrubbing the conditioner out of my hair and face so I can open my eyes.

No response.

I then feel two hands rubbing my back with soap. This is freaky. I get the last of the conditioner off my face and spin around, ready to face the person who trespassed into my domain. Nobody is there!

Someone is playing a joke on me. "Not funny." But nobody responds. "You can show yourself now." But nobody appears. I then see a washcloth rise into the air in front of me. I move my hands above it to try to find the strings that raised it in the air, but there are no strings. The hair stands up on the back of my neck.

Next, the soap rises in the air, too. Then the washcloth rubs the soap. I see the washcloth approach me, on level with my belly button, and start cleaning my belly! Gentle circles, and then it backs away, and I see more soap is rubbed against it. The washcloth comes back, this time doing the same pattern on my chest and shoulders. Each breast is scrubbed in the same small circular pattern.

This is crazy, but it also arouses me to get scrubbed by an invisible person. A ghost! I give in to the floating cloth and turn around so my back can be completely cleaned. The washcloth starts at my shoulders and then works its way down. I feel a large rough hand on my shoulder to steady me as the washcloth scrubs my back, working down to my bottom. He applies the circular pattern against my bottom with more pressure than he did on my back. "Yum," I whisper, spreading my legs apart slightly.

The ghost scrubs the backs of my legs and my thighs. The hand on my shoulder leaves me and an arm wraps around my belly. I am gently pulled back toward a male body. I know it is a male for obvious reasons. I feel the washcloth scrubbing between my legs. Ahhh. While scrubbing there, the thumb on the hand holding me around my belly stretches up and gently tickles my nipple. Ooooh.

"Yes," is the only word I can let out, but too soon the washcloth drops to the shower floor, and I know I am by myself again. I finish rinsing off the suds and turn off the water. I take my thick white towel from behind the door and dry myself before leaving the shower stall. Then I wrap it tightly around myself, so it resembles a white tube dress. I walk past my bed to the dresser to grab a pair of undies.

As I brush past my bed, I feel two large hands grab my waist. Startled, I turn around to see who grabbed me, yet see no one there. I know it is my ghost.

He pulls me back toward him and even through my towel, I can feel his shaft against my bottom. He is sitting on my bed and, while keeping his hands on my waist, lifts me up. I feel his legs part my thighs, and he places me over his shaft and slowly lets me down. I feel him enter me. I can tell he is well endowed, because I am still high off the bed and he is already inside of me.

He gently lowers me all of the way down, so I am sitting completely on his lap, his shaft fully inside me. My level of arousal is off the charts.

"I guess I do owe you for the shower," I say, enjoying this immensely.

Then he lifts me up a few inches and down I go, up and down. Slowly at first and then much faster. My "oohs" and "ahhs" are the only sounds heard, and I realize how weird it is to fuck a ghost. Or more precisely, to be fucked by a ghost. He is making no sounds, but I can tell by the quick movements up and down that the ghost must be enjoying this, too.

I know he has climaxed as I feel him shoot inside of me. The ride is coming to an end. He lifts me up and down a few more times in slow motion before settling me down again on his shaft.

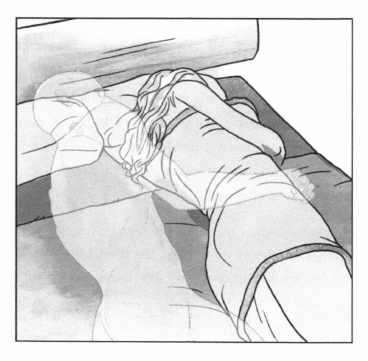

He then lies down on my bed, holding me snugly from behind. He is still inside of me, one arm wrapped tightly around my waist.

The sun woke me up, shining through the venetian blinds. I moved slowly, trying not to stir the sleeping ghost beside me. Then I realized it was just me under the covers.

What an awesome dream! That sneaky Siyo took my fantasy and made it real. Well, maybe not real, but that dream felt real.

Wait a minute – I have never had sex before. Did I lose my virginity in my dream? Impossible. You cannot lose your virginity in a dream.

How did I know how to have sex? Actually, I did not know how to have sex, the ghost did all of the work. I just went along for the ride.

Had Siyo seen me naked as the controller of this dream? I didn't know, but I guessed the controller could see all. I felt exposed thinking that Siyo most likely saw me in my birthday suit.

The euphoric feeling I felt after this dream had evaporated. Keeping my ghost fantasy a secret made it special I realized, but to have it acted out in my dream made this fantasy seem insignificant. I also didn't know Siyo's part, but if he did see me naked, maybe we should take a break from this dream snatcher for a while.

Raw Oysters

Living near the Jersey shore, I have easy access to fresh oysters. People believe that oysters are aphrodisiacs, and I know from one of my biology classes that there is a scientific reason for this – oysters contain amino acids, which trigger the production of sex hormones. The more oysters, well, you know, the more…sex.

This is a two-sentence easy recipe!

Clean the oysters under cold running water and then carefully cut the muscle from the shell and remove any small pieces of shell or sediment. Flip the oyster over in its juices and serve immediately.

For added amore, serve the oysters with red wine. Red wine contains resveratrol, an antioxidant that helps boost blood flow and improves circulation before and during intercourse.

Beam Me Up

Siyo and I dated regularly after that first date, and he even asked me out to our senior prom. We competed more in mini-golf, in the games along the Seaside boardwalk, and in the arcade.

I enjoyed walking along the boardwalk the most. Growing up near the Jersey shore meant spending many Sundays as a kid exploring the wonders of the Point Pleasant and Seaside boardwalks with my parents. There is a picture of me in a small silver frame on my parents' nightstand taken at the Point Pleasant boardwalk – I have a candy apple in one hand and a stuffed animal in the other hand that my dad won for me at one of the many boardwalk games.

Siyo and I are both competitive, but Siyo would resort to cheating in order to win. During our second mini-golf match, I caught him pushing the ball slightly with his foot toward the hole when he thought I wasn't looking.

"Siyo, you get a five-point penalty for cheating."

"What? What are you talking about? I didn't do anything."

"I saw you move the ball with your foot. Don't deny it."

"You're seeing things, Jenn. Just because I'm beating you by three points, you are looking for reasons for why you're not winning."

I huffed and crossed my arms. Siyo laughed, probably because I resembled an angry child. I felt angry though. There is a difference between cheating and competing. I made sure I won that game, and then Siyo crossed his arms.

"Why do you have to be so competitive?" Siyo asked after I beat him by two points.

"I like to win. Don't be such a sore loser, just because you have to buy me ice cream. In fact, if you don't snap out of it, I am going to order Blizzards for my mom and dad, too, your treat."

Siyo forced out a laugh.

For several dates, I stopped asking about the dream snatcher and never even mentioned the ghost dream to Siyo. I also never asked for a free dream as an incentive for beating him at a game.

Siyo on the other hand, with his competitive nature, set incentives for everything we did.

"If I can knock down all of the bottles with just one ball, you have to French kiss me."

"If I beat you in pinball, you have to let us walk for at least a block with my hand in your back pocket."

"If I get a hole-in-one on this hole, I get three tries to guess the color of your underwear."

He always had a sexual-related incentive ready for every game. I sometimes liked the attention as well as the additional competition driven by his mischievous motivation, but I often felt he prioritized physical contact with me over trying to get to know me better. Once, after we walked for a few minutes with his hand snug in my back pocket, I asked him, "Siyo, do you know what I want to study in college?"

"I don't have a clue. I know you are going to the College of New Jersey, which is nearby, so we can continue to date. What you study is your business."

"Okay, answer this question – who are my three closest friends?"

Some hesitation. "I see you sometimes with that short blonde, what's her name? And then there's that tall brunette. She's hot." He stopped quickly when he saw the look I gave him.

"Amy," I said and removed his hand from my back pocket. We walked side by side, not even holding hands.

We filled in the awkward gaps of silence with talking about who's taking who to the prom and which beaches to hang out at during the summer. I realized while we were talking that I find Siyo handsome and fun to be with, but at this point in our relationship I don't love him and I know he doesn't love me. He values lust over love, simple as that. Maybe all boys do, at least high school boys. I had overheard boys talking about "scoring." I have no doubt he too, participated in these conversations and had having sex as one of his top high school goals. I would imagine there is more to a relationship than fucking, not that I would know. French kissing is as far as I've ever gone.

Siyo seemed so friendly though. It can take time to love someone — we've only dated a couple of weeks. *Give it some more time,* my heart told my brain. My brain wasn't convinced.

"Siyo, what does your name mean?" By the silence that followed, I could tell that this question surprised him. If he had no interest in me beyond my skin, maybe I should get more interested in him, and then he would take an interest in me.

"The name Siyo is short for Siyotanka, which means 'flute' in Lakota, the language spoken within my Sioux tribe. There are not many people from my tribe left. Once a year, we have a family reunion, and every year less and less people go. This past year, there must have been at most thirty of us. As a child, I remember hundreds going." He continued talking enthusiastically about his tribe.

Maybe a connection existed between his name and his strong sexual drive. Thinking only about my appearance, wanting to physically touch me, wanting to have sex with me. Siyo meaning flute. Flute could have more than one meaning, too, as it could be a phallic symbol. Flute equaled penis. He thought with his penis.

I realized he finished talking, and we walked for a while quietly side by side.

"I'm yearbook photographer this year, you know." Siyo broke the silence.

"I didn't know that. I know picture week is next week and I have been shopping for a dress for my yearbook picture with my mom for several days. We went to over a dozen stores before we found the right one."

"What does the *right one* look like?" Siyo asked, trying to make conversation.

He finally asked something about me, or at least about my dress. "It's pink. One of my favorite colors. Did you know that, Siyo?"

Siyo ignored my question. "Is it a hot dress?"

"Maybe without the jacket. The jacket makes it a little more formal. The skirt goes up to here." I put my hand just below my knees. "It is kind of frilly, too. I'll be wearing white shoes — it should look nice."

"The dress doesn't sound too hot. I guess if you picked it out with your mom, it can't be too hot."

"My dress on the hot scale is smack between what Archie's Veronica would wear and *Jersey Shore*'s Snooki." I found this funny and laughed but Siyo stayed quiet so I continued. "You know I'm not a slut, Siyo. There are plenty of girls who are, and I'm sure they'll be wearing close to nothing for these pictures. In fact, maybe you would be happier with one of those sluts than with me. Maybe you should ask Amy to go to the prom with you instead of me." He reacted quickly to my frustration.

"Hey, hey, Jenn. I like being with you. I'm sure the dress is pretty. Don't get so touchy."

I crossed my arms and the rest of the date consisted of awkward silence or forced conversation.

Siyo loved photography and planned to take pictures of all of the high school seniors for the yearbook. Not the formal headshots, which a professional photograph took, but the fun pictures taken around the school and town. Many of us high school seniors got dressed in formal outfits and took pictures outside at a nearby university, which had once been a mansion for a wealthy businessman. The university grounds contained many beautiful sculptures and fountains.

We took my yearbook pictures right after school. Siyo wanted me to sit on the edge of a fountain, which had several ornate steps. I sat on the second step, with one foot on the first step, and the other foot on the grass. He stood several feet away with his camera.

"Now move your arm. No not like that. Here." He walked over to me and moved my arm so it rested on my knees. He placed my other hand over my arm. He turned my shoulders slightly.

"This position isn't so comfortable," I said.

"It's not supposed to be. But it is supposed to be a good shot. I know poses."

He made me feel like a famous model posing during a shoot.

He took a few pictures of me.

"Jenn, your lips look a little dry. Can you just lick around your lips a few times?"

I let my tongue slowly work its way around my lips.

He said, "That's better."

"You're too serious." I stuck my tongue out at him. He grinned and took a picture. "I better not see that one go anywhere."

"Just for my own personal collection. You know how I like that tongue."

"Your mind is in the gutter." Siyo was thinking with his flute.

"Now raise your skirt just a bit."

Now Siyo was definitely thinking with his flute. "Come again?" I responded.

"The skirt is a little creased, and I don't want the creases to appear in the photo. Just pull it up a little bit, Jenn. Don't be a prude. This will make a better photo. Trust me."

Even if Siyo had dubious motives, I did want a good picture. If he noticed creases, I wanted to hide them. I pulled up my skirt just a little bit.

"Good, good." I heard the camera shutter as he continued to take pictures.

"Now it would look even better," he continued, "without that pink jacket."

I closed my eyes and sighed.

"That jacket is something your mom would wear," he taunted.

That strung a chord with me. My mom had helped me pick out this outfit. "Do you think so?"

"Definitely. Lose the jacket. Here, allow me." He put down his camera and walked over to me. He helped me remove the jacket and folded it neatly, putting it on his camera case so it would not come into contact with the grass. He then came back and moved me into position again, this time touching my bare shoulders. I shivered slightly. Before going back to his camera, he hesitated for a moment, and then pulled up my skirt, at least by another six inches.

"What are you doing?"

"You know how important yearbook picture are, Jenn. Don't you want every guy twenty years from now to look back at this yearbook and say, 'Wow, who's that girl?'"

"That's from a song. You didn't make that phrase up. Besides, my parents are going to be looking at my yearbook."

"I'll tell you what. I will show you all of the pictures I take, and you can decide which one makes the yearbook. The other ones will go into my personal photo collection."

I stuck out my tongue again, and he quickly hit the shutter, capturing the moment.

"I want to try a different type of shot now, so bear with me." He walked back to me. "I'd like you to lean back and put your head down like this." He gently tilted my head.

"Take the pictures quick. All of the blood is rushing to my head."

"That's what I like." He continued to take pictures. "It makes it look like you are blushing."

It took me a moment to realize that with my head back and no jacket, he had a perfect view of my cleavage and who knew what else. Before I completely realized this, he took a bunch of pictures. I sat up quickly and started blushing for real.

"Enough," I said.

He put his camera down and came over and French kissed me.

"Do you do that to all the girls you photograph for the yearbook?"

He didn't stir and kept his gaze fixed on me. He didn't even seem to blink. I imagined him a wolf in another life and me his prey. I broke eye contact with him and looked at my shoes instead. They were white suede shoes with shiny brass buckles. I kept staring at the buckles, hoping he would say something to fill in the silence. His wolf hungered.

Finally, in desperation, I broke the silence. "What position do you want me in now?"

He hesitated for a minute, but I knew my question stirred something in him, as I could see his shaft protrude against his Dockers, like a piling being raised under a miniature circus tent.

"Your mind remains in the gutter. I mean, what other pictures should we take? I have homework to do."

But he ignored me and his inner wolf attacked me, his prey. Siyo bent down and kissed me again. And again. I felt something deep in my belly, and I, under his spell, kissed him back.

"What are we doing?" I asked him nervously.

"Whatever comes after kissing," he responded, trying to sound sure of himself, but I could hear the anxious tone in his voice.

"How do you know what comes after kissing?" I asked.

He didn't answer. Siyo took my hands and pulled me up from sitting on the fountain edge. He then stepped over the waist-high fountain walls and helped me over into the large blue cement bowl, which at some point in history had been filled with water. We stood in an empty fountain, looking at each other, not sure what to do next.

He pushed me down by my shoulders so we were both hidden behind the fountain walls. His wolf attacked me once again. Rough French kissing, and he started grabbing my private parts. He pressed one hand against my breast and the other on my bottom, clumsily and roughly rubbing and squeezing my body while French kissing me.

"That hurts, not so rough." But the wolf ignored the rabbit. He continued to aggressively grope me.

It felt weird to have him touching my breast and bottom, even through my clothes. The tips of my nipples became hard, and my heart rate increased. What next? Should there be anything next, or should we stop here? I imagined my mom watching. What would she expect me to do? My mom and I picked out this dress and now Siyo's paws were all over it, in all of the places where a boy's hands should never tread.

Siyo continued letting his hands freely explore my body over my new dress while he remained locked to my lips, and I awkwardly rubbed my hands over the front of his pants, trying to think what my mom would say.

"Now, Jennifer," she would start. She always called me "Jennifer" before saying something serious. "You are only a virgin once. Save it for someone you love."

Siyo tried pulling down my panties and tights while kissing me, but did not have much success. He released his lips from mine and his hands from my body and growled, "Take your clothes off."

We both sat down and took off our shoes. We were hidden from the outside world as the walls of the fountain surrounded us so nobody could see. The shadows from the sun lit up slivers of the blue-painted cement, which peeled off in many places. I felt like we were doing something illegal, something that we shouldn't be doing, something sneaky, and these feelings further aroused me.

With my lips unlocked from his, I spoke. "Maybe this is not such a good idea. We are outside, and we have not done this before. I know we are not ready.

Aren't we supposed to wait until we get married? I could get my dress dirty, and my parents would know what we did and my dad would cut off your you-know-what..."

Siyo ignored me and despite my reservations, I allowed him to pull down my tights and underwear. I then watched Siyo as he took off his pants and then his underwear.

We kept our tops on. We didn't discuss with each other why, but if someone saw us by peering over the top of the fountain, at least we would appear to have all of our clothes on. Also, we were anxious enough just taking off our underwear in front of each other.

Siyo sat on the cold painted blue cement fountain floor. I saw his penis for the first time, which pointed directly at me. I started giggling and then advanced to snorting and could not stop.

"Hey, you know what that does to a guy's ego?" Siyo asked, joining in with a laugh and making this serious situation seem silly.

"I have never seen one of those before."

"This is an extra-large size. Most of them are small, maybe a quarter of this size," Siyo bragged.

I just nodded, and kept laughing.

"Do you have one of those wiener caps?" I asked him.

"Yes, but I have never put one on before." Siyo took out a gray condom wrapper from his wallet. His hand shook slightly. "I hope it is still good. It has been in my wallet since the day after I sat next to you in Spanish. I thought of this moment for a long time." He handed me the condom, his penis still pointing at me, and the wolf frozen.

"Let's see if we can figure this out," I said. I tore open the condom wrapper and pulled out a yellow ring covered with plastic on top. The material felt like a balloon and smelled like one, too.

I put it over his penis. "I guess it goes like this," I said, while trying to push it down over his shaft. It didn't move. "Maybe it goes the other way." I took the condom off and put it on the other way, and sure enough, I pulled it down and unwrapped the sides of it to completely cover his shaft.

"Don't touch him so much," Siyo said, squirming slightly. "He is too excited already. He is almost ready now."

By *he*, I knew this is how Siyo referred to his penis. "Okay, step one complete," I said, trying to be funny and hide my anxiety. Siyo's nervousness showed. He sat frozen on the cold cement bottom of the fountain, not sure what to do next.

"Okay, on to step two," I continued. "You stay seated on the ground like you are doing." I pulled up my dress and put my legs around him, so I sat on his lap facing him, my legs apart, inches away from his shaft. I kissed him gently on the lips.

"Okay, if we are going to do this, now would probably be a good time." With that, I held his shaft with one hand and scooted myself closer on his lap, inserting him into my sex. I gasped and he let out a sound resembling a growl. His wolf returned.

"Is it in?" Siyo asked.

"You don't feel it?" I asked back.

"It can go in further." Siyo then put in hands on my backside and pulled me closer to him.

"Go slow," I whispered.

His wolf ignored my request and kept pulling me closer to him, his shaft going deeper and deeper inside of me until our bellies almost touched.

"This feels awesome," Siyo said as he gave me a small kiss on the lips. I felt pain as he pushed himself in, but did not let him see this on my face, as I wanted this first time to be special for both of us.

I put my arms around him and kissed him back, a much harder kiss. "It's not over yet, mister," I said, moving my thighs back and forth a little bit.

"Keep doing that, but go slower," Siyo said. "He is right on the edge." He had an expression of complete euphoric shock. His eyes were closed, and his neck stretched back a little bit.

I continued to go back and forth, his jittery and now sweaty hands clamped to my butt.

It felt bizarre to have a penis inside of me. It barely fit, and I could imagine it felt better for him than it did for me. "You've got to work, too," I told him. "Move your butt up and down."

"I can't," Siyo said. "I will scrape myself against the cement. You are doing fine. Keep moving like you are moving. No wait, stop moving. Stop moving!"

But it was too late. "Oh no, oh no, oh no," Siyo kept yelling.

"Shhhh, be quiet," I said and kissed him to keep him quiet. "Nobody can know we are here."

He said nothing else, but just had a goofy expression on his face as his spasms continued for a few more moments before he finally stilled. With the wolf satisfied, I found myself no longer his prey. We were Jenn and Siyo again.

I pretended to be cool. "Short and sweet," I said and pecked him on the lips. "Congratulations, we are both no longer virgins. Let's get dressed pronto and get out of this fountain."

I got off of him and quickly put back on my underwear and tights.

"What do I do now?" asked Siyo, looking at his slightly deflated penis with a balloon full of liquid around it.

"You're on your own now." I stepped back over the fountain wall.

"Love 'em and leave 'em," Siyo said with the same goofy smile on his face.

I walked away, leaving my virginity behind somewhere in that fountain.

I felt sad. I couldn't put my finger on why I felt down. Maybe because losing my virginity meant crossing another threshold in life, or I had anticipated the first time would be more romantic than screwing in an empty fountain, or maybe I simply did not expect to lose my virginity with Siyo. This last thought bothered me the most. I liked Siyo, but I did not love him yet, and my mom's imaginary words kept playing again and again in my head: *Save it for someone you love.* I didn't love Siyo. I'd never loved anyone outside my family and pets before. I considered him special to me, and a good friend, but shouldn't there be more?

"Jenn, I will always remember that," Siyo said, catching up to me while tucking his shirt back into his pants.

"I have to go home now," I replied.

"Hey, before you leave, a present."

I turned around as he took the dream snatcher out of his camera case. "Can I treat you to a free dream? I promise you'll like it."

Did Siyo travel everywhere with a condom and his dream snatcher? Did I need another dream? I hadn't brought up the dream snatcher since that ghost dream because I didn't want to open myself up completely to Siyo both mentally and of course physically. He must have seen me naked in the ghost dream. But we just had sex in an empty fountain. He had seen me almost completely naked just now. I did enjoy that last dream. "Okay, but make it a good one."

Siyo stretched his hand out, and I put my hand in his. He reopened my paper cut again with the same sharp edge of the tool and I twitched. "Ouch."

He had no sympathy for my pain. "Don't worry, it will be worth it," Siyo said and took out a Band-Aid.

When I got back home that day, my parents asked how the photo shoot went.

"I hope we created some nice memories," I said, letting my parents read into it what they wanted.

"That is such a pretty dress," my mom said. *Don't dust it for fingerprints. You will find Siyo's paw prints everywhere on it.* I did not say this out loud.

"Siyo is such a respectable young boy," my dad said. *You would not think that if you knew what he did to your daughter today.* Of course, I did not say that out loud either.

I finished my homework after dinner and afterwards watched an old *Star Trek* episode on Netflix with my parents. I felt tired and yet also excited to get to sleep and see what dream awaited.

"Captain Jenn, there appears to be a life form on the planet below. Galaxy Command told us this planet could not support life, but this is obviously not the case."

I swivel my commander chair around to face my first officer. Everyone on the bridge waits for my response. "Prepare the teleporter. I will beam down to the planet and see what is down there." He nods and leaves the bridge. I stand up, looking out the ship's window, seeing thousands of stars and what Galaxy Command thought to be a cold lifeless planet below.

I also see my reflection in the window. My captain's uniform consists of a 1960s vintage curve-hugging turtleneck with black slacks. Stripper meets Captain Kirk is how I would describe my attire.

I grab my phasor and head to the teleporter. Within seconds, I am standing in an open field on this strange planet. My phasor is drawn.

"Approximately 400 feet to your right is the life form," my first officer from the bridge tells me.

"Over and out." I start walking, unsure of whether the alien is friendly or not.

I reach the spot where there should be an alien, yet see nothing that appears to be alive. I am about to notify the bridge that there is no life on the planet, when something grabs my ankles from behind.

I spin around, easily freeing myself and look down with my phasor aimed directly at the head of a nervous monkey.

The monkey shrieks and starts stepping back.

I chuckle and lower the gun. "First Officer, this is Captain Jenn. There is only a harmless monkey..." Before I could finish my sentence, the monkey charges me.

He jumps up at me, his face collides with my breasts and his long hairy arms hold on tight around my arms and waist as I fall backward on the ground. I could not free my arms to cushion the fall and so I land square on my butt.

"You son-of-a…," I say as I reach for my phasor, but I don't finish my sentence.

The monkey is over me now, holding my gun as if it is a banana. He tries biting it and then gives up and hurls it far away.

He starts smelling me all over, starting with my neck. He has me pinned to the sandy ground. His nose makes its way over my chests and belly and then to my private area below my belly button. He takes a deep breath there.

He rubs his furry hands over my slacks, in between my legs and on my backside. He tugs at my slacks until my panties are visible. Then he pulls both my panties and slacks down to my knees, and is now looking at my sex. He scratches his head again.

I try to get up, but he has me pinned. He then gently rubs his hand over my small soft hairs and then moves my legs apart slightly and lowers his head down to my sex. It tickles slightly as he takes several deep breaths. Then I feel something that tickles even more – his tongue!

This is all new to me and I feel him lick me down there, all over back and forth. His hands keep my legs apart as he appears to be cleaning me down there. I try to pull him off of me. His licking affects my body. My body tightens and frustration is building.

"Please stop, that feels weird," I plead but the monkey keeps licking. With each lick, my body further tightens. "No, no, oh, oh!"

"Captain, are you okay?" my worried first officer asks through my teleporter device.

I scream at the peak of my body's tightness. When I do, the monkey stops and looks at me and scratches his head again.

It takes me a few moments to collect myself and pull up my panties and slacks. I scoop up the monkey and try to regain my composure as I talk into the teleporter.

"Everything is fine, First Officer. I found a pet on this planet, one that I will be taking up with me. He possesses a talent that I need to explore further. Prepare to beam us both back."

An alarm is sounding when we both arrived back on the ship.

"Enemy ship!" someone yells. I quickly start making my way back to the bridge, holding the monkey like a small child, the monkey's head nestled on my bosom. The alarm gets louder and louder as I make my way to the bridge.

The alarm woke me up. Morning already? I quickly turned the alarm off, and stared at the ceiling a few moments.

I lost my virginity yesterday and last night had an orgasm in my dream. I felt more like a woman than a girl. I had never had an orgasm before. If that's what it felt like to have an orgasm, I want more of these – lots more.

Bananas, Strawberries and Almonds, Oh My!

I never say "no" to chocolate, especially dark chocolate. The darker the better. Give me 85% cocoa over 50% any day. I always feel good after eating dark chocolate, and a little research online revealed why. Dark chocolate contains dopamine and phenylethylamine, which together give us a feeling of euphoria.

What do I like to dip in the chocolate? Besides my fingers, I love to dip bananas, strawberries, and almonds. Not only do these fruit taste great in chocolate, bananas and strawberries can definitely put you in the mood. What do bananas look like?

Okay, now that you have the visual, bananas contain the enzyme bromelain, which triggers testosterone production. Bananas also contain plenty of vitamin B, which increases energy, so you can go that extra mile in the sheets.

Dip strawberries, too. Strawberries are just such a sexy-looking fruit. Under their sensual juicy skin, they are packed with vitamin C, which helps blood flow to all parts of the body.

And don't forget the almonds! Almonds have always been regarded as fertility symbols. The smell of almond has been proven to arouse passion in females – it works with me.

Melt chocolate using a double boiler or two sauce pans, then wash the fruit and dip it in the chocolate and let it cool in the fridge on a cookie sheet. Dip almonds just halfway in the chocolate. It makes them look fancy and allows you to easily hold them while dipping.

My Best ASSet

I interviewed for a waitress job at the Ridge diner. The Ridge is just a few miles from my house, and my parents and I have eaten there about once a month for as long as I can remember. Diners were invented in New Jersey, and it is no surprise therefore in my opinion that the best diners are in New Jersey as well.

I had worked part-time jobs since turning fourteen. Not because my family needed the money or because I needed to save up for the quantity of Blizzards I needed to buy Siyo whenever he beat me in mini-golf, but because I knew work benefited both the mind and the body, especially the body. All of the on-your-feet type of jobs I had taken over the years, such as working at a food stand at Great Adventure or being a hostess at a Charlie Brown's restaurant, had strengthened and toned my body. This waitress job would require a similar level of endurance. Being on my feet built up muscles, which eventually supported eye-turning curves.

I wore the dress that I wore for the yearbook picture, the pink one with the frills and Siyo's invisible paw prints, along with the accompanying jacket. I felt nervous for my interview, but I had always found that the nervous energy helped me do even better. I shook hands with John, the owner of the diner, a stout, balding middle-aged man. We sat at one of the small booths and talked.

"Would you like some coffee?" he asked me.

"No, thank you, I'm okay."

He signaled for a waitress to bring him a cup. "So tell me about yourself."

I hated these types of open-ended questions, but at least someone is interested in me. "My name is Jenn Bradley, I am a high school senior graduating in a couple of months. I am going to the College of New Jersey in the fall and looking for a job where I can save some money for school. I can work around my high school schedule until I graduate, and then this summer I can work many more hours. I am a hard worker."

John took a sip from his coffee and checked something on his iPhone. He ignored me and showed no interest in my responses after all. My pulse quickened as I forced myself to contain my frustration. "I am good at memorizing what people order, and I am also good at balancing plates and cups. I am strong. I get along well with others." I hesitated for a minute and then added, "I haven't killed anyone this week."

He didn't raise his eyebrows or say anything in surprise, which confirmed that he did not care what I said.

"Good, good," he said. I maintained my professional composure and restrained myself from sticking my tongue out at him.

"What is your best asset?"

"My best asset is definitely my ass, Mr. John. During foreplay, the first place men's hands usually grab is my ass. I have been told it makes for great handles during rough sex."

"Good, good." John continued studying his iPhone. "We have several shifts open immediately. You will need to work both Friday and Saturday nights. Is that a problem?"

I thought how this might impact my social life with Siyo. He would understand though. Besides, I could definitely use the money for school, and Friday and Saturday nights the restaurant should be more crowded, so I will make more in tips. "No, I can work the weekend no problem. When can I start?"

"Be here at five on Saturday. You will need at least an hour to follow around Paul, who has been a waiter here for many years, and learn the ropes." He pointed to Paul, who waited on a table near us. "Let me get your waitress uniform." John went into the back.

I could not hide my excitement. I have never been a waitress before. John returned a minute later with an outfit on a hanger protected by a thin plastic dry cleaning bag. "Here you go, Ms. Jenn. Welcome aboard." He introduced me to Paul on the way out.

I called Siyo as soon as I got into the car. "Fantastic news, Siyo. I got the waitress job!"

"What hours do you have to work?"

"A few shifts during the week, but I will need to work both Friday and Saturday nights." He did not respond so I continued. "Siyo, I need the money for college."

"When can we see each other then?"

"On Sundays. And it's not like we don't see each other in school."

"What if I ask Amy out for Friday or Saturday night? I don't want to sit home alone."

"Take her to my diner for a date. I can wait on you and hopefully you will give me a well-deserved big tip." This ended the conversation.

On Saturday, I got dressed into my uniform. The outfit consisted of a white blouse, black vest, and skintight black spandex pants. I thought the pants would split when I sat down in my car to drive there, but luckily they didn't. When I entered the diner, I went up to John and commented on the outfit. "These pants are too tight. Do you have a larger size?"

"Sorry, Jenn, those are the ones you wear. Remember this, the more curves you show, the more food we sell."

I shook my head and he continued, "Besides, you did divulge your greatest asset to me, and now everyone can admire it."

I felt the redness on my face as I blushed. "So you were listening."

"Every word. Why do you think I hired you so fast?" John let out a hearty Santa Claus laugh which shook his whole round body. I liked John, and knew he could take some back-and-forth.

"Why don't the men wear pants like this as well? If waitresses wear spandex, waiters should, too. Paul would look hot in tight spandex pants." I knew this gave John an awful visual, as Paul weighed over 300 pounds.

"Paul is ready for you," he said while reaching for his iPhone, and I knew this meant the end of the conversation.

After a long first week of waitressing, I experienced the advantages of wearing spandex. The kitchen could easily get over 100 degrees with the food cooking, so wearing thin clothes when picking up orders had its benefits. Also, I experienced that "the more curves you show, the more tips" as well.

Many of my customers were men dining alone. This diner, because of its proximity to two major highways, the Garden State Parkway and the New Jersey Turnpike, catered to people driving through Jersey, including many truck drivers going north to New York or south to Delaware.

In addition to the positive correlation between curves and tips, I quickly learned a second positive correlation between conversation and tips. The more I chatted with customers, the more money I made. I had become good at listening and talking with men. I had also become skilled in pretending to listen, which although is not as good as actually listening, still led to more tips. I perfected a silly laugh that I used whenever I had no idea what someone had said and I just wanted to politely end the conversation.

I took their orders, I served them their food, I made casual conversation, and all the while I felt like a model doing the catwalk from the kitchen to their tables and back again. Sometimes I felt certain guys purposely made me walk several times to their table, just so they could watch me walk away from them.

"Ma'am can you bring me some relish for my hot dog?"

"Sure thing."

"Sorry to bother you again, miss, but can I also have some extra napkins? I am an awful messy eater," the customer would say after I put the relish down on this table.

"No problem." I knew where his eyes have been and where they would go again.

My second day on the job, I dropped a handful of napkins and made the mistake of bending over to pick them up with my back to several men at a nearby booth. If those men's eyes were laser beams, my pants would have been just a few smoking shreds of spandex on the floor and my rump would have burnt to resemble a ripe Jersey tomato. One man whistled, which made me blush, and the conversations I overheard several of those men having with each other after this incident were in poor taste.

"What I could do with that," one overweight gray-bearded man told the other horny men with him. I heard some chuckles and similarly vulgar comments afterward.

On a positive note, I got great tips that evening. If I could ignore my self-conscious, I would strategically drop napkins on a regular basis.

Another time, I left the kitchen with my order and the cook yelled, "Hey, you got some butter on your ass." I guess I'd sat on one of those little diner packets of butter, or rubbed against some butter while cleaning a table.

I responded automatically. "Maybe I'll get better tips." And that evening, I actually did!

On my second Saturday night shift, Siyo walked in with Amy, my friend who Siyo considered hot. My face flushed when I saw them. Siyo pointed to me as the hostess grabbed two menus and led them to my area.

"Hi, Jenn, we decided to stop by and see you," Siyo said, grinning. He didn't hold hands with Amy or do anything else which would have confirmed they were on a date.

"Hi, guys," I replied, smiling back.

"Hi, Jenn," Amy said. "I come to this diner a lot with my parents. The best rice pudding in the world!" She appeared genuinely happy to be here and see me.

"What would you recommend?" Siyo asked, pretending to be reading through the menu.

'The ravioli is good, and Amy is right, the rice pudding cannot be beat." For some reason, it didn't upset me that Siyo came here with Amy. I knew Siyo did this to bother me, and maybe that's why it didn't bother me at all. Maybe I didn't feel jealous because I didn't love Siyo.

Siyo continued to try to push my buttons. "What would you like, sweetie?" he asked Amy.

Sweetie? I had never considered Amy a *Sweetie*. She would definitely be a *Foxy*.

"I'll have the ravioli and of course rice pudding for dessert," Amy said.

"Good choice. And you, Siyo?"

"Burger and fries, no pickle. If there's a pickle, I'll give it back."

I flashed Siyo a look that made his smile break, but only for a moment. I then smiled at both of them. "Be back shortly."

I placed their order and continued to focus on my customers instead of on my heart, which had started to hurt. *Brain over heart, brain over heart, I don't love Siyo,* I reminded myself.

Siyo and Amy stayed a long time after eating, which annoyed me for two reasons. They must be enjoying each other's company, but more importantly, with both of them parked in this booth, I couldn't get new customers to sit there and so my tips were impacted.

When they finally left, Siyo did not even leave me a tip! Just a short note which said *Tip = free dream.*

I stopped by his house after my shift, close to midnight and luckily no Amy.

"Did you enjoy seeing us?" Siyo grinned.

"You made my night. Are you and Amy dating? If yes, we're through."

"No, we are not dating. You are always so touchy. You told me I should stop by with her. We just wanted to see you, that is all. Besides, I wanted to give you a nice dream. If we can't date on the weekends, at least we can date in our dreams, can't we?"

"Maybe," I said. "What kind of dream do you have in mind?"

"I haven't thought of it fully, yet. Maybe a tough police officer or a detective – a position where you are in charge. What do you think?"

A position of authority appealed to me. "No horny monkeys, agreed?"

"Agreed." Siyo walked into his bedroom and removed the dream snatcher from the dresser. "Give me your hand."

I gave him my hand and he callously cut me. The same sharp pain in the same place. He didn't have a Band-Aid handy, so I told him I would wrap it when I got home.

I got home after midnight.

As I walked from my car to the front door, the only sounds were the clapping of my heels against the asphalt driveway pavement. I opened and closed the door quietly, careful not to wake my parents.

A small nightlight in the living room dimly lit the entranceway. I slid my finger between my shoe and heel of each foot and placed my shoes neatly by the door. If my feet could talk, they would give a sigh of relief to be free from the uncomfortable high heels.

I tiptoed into the kitchen, got a glass from above the sink, filled it about halfway with tap water, and retired to my bedroom. With the door safely shut, I turned on the ceiling fan light. It took a few moments for my eyes to adjust to the bright light.

I emptied my front and back pockets on the bed. Lots of scrunched-up bills, mostly dollars but some fives and a couple of tens, too. Tens were good, I liked tens. The green paper tumbleweeds on my white comforter were a reminder to myself that next time I should fold the bills neater before shoving them into my pockets. The bills could rip or worse, fall out. Still, the mounds of paper looked much more substantial than a neatly folded stack.

One day, if I hit the jackpot or make a massive amount of tips during a shift, I will cover my comforter with crumpled-up bills and roll completely au naturel back and forth over them, like Demi Moore in *Indecent Proposal*.

Reality check. I'm not Demi Moore, I'm Jenn Bradley, a full-time high school student and part-time waitress, saving tip money for college. One day, I will have a psychology degree and could analyze my own rolling in dirty bills fetish, but right now I needed to get out of my waitress duds.

My waitress outfit reeked of the smell of fried foods. After a while, you get used to this smell. Smelling grease sometimes makes we want to take food orders. This would make a great psychology study – the positive effects of greasy food smells on waitresses. I read about a classical conditioning study where a bell rang before feeding a dog. The dog would start salivating whenever he heard the bell, knowing food will be served. After a while, the dog started salivating when the bell rang, even in the absence of food. Maybe if I kept waitressing long enough, I would start salivating whenever I smelled grease.

I undressed down to my bra and panties, and put my waitress uniform in a white plastic garbage bag that my mom left on my bed. I closed the bag so it did not smell up everything else in the room and my mom would wash it tomorrow.

I walked into the bathroom connected to my bedroom and turned on the light. Off came my bra and panties and into the hamper they went. I glanced at my backside in the mirror and noticed three oval-shaped red marks, resembling large mosquito bites.

A seasoned waitress warned me on my first day that some customers get their jollies from pinching butts. She would discreetly identify to me the regular butt pinchers. Despite her advice, I had been pinched on average twice during each shift, and three times tonight. I had never been pinched before taking this job, and I didn't like the surprise or the pain. Although I felt violated whenever a horny man's fingers compressed tightly on my sensitive skin, I never reacted and just took it as part of the job. If I complained, I might get in trouble with the owner or worse, it might impact tips.

I took a hot shower and scrubbed off all of the diner smells. I toweled myself dry and it felt great to be clean once again. Thoughts of sleep entered my mind as I brushed my teeth and flossed.

I pulled a pair of underwear from the top drawer and my pajamas from the second drawer. I loved the PJs with footsies, and the flower-patterned flannel ones I put on made me feel like a kid again. I got cozy under the covers and wondered what Siyo had in store for me tonight. I wouldn't mind being a detective.

I am laying on my stomach on a large rock overlooking a crystal clear lake. I am gazing out over the lake in a meditative state. My hair is down, and I am wearing a spandex long sleeve shirt designed for yoga, over skintight jeans.

"Is she on her way?" I whisper into my iPhone.

Siyo's anxious voice responds. "We think so. Remember Jenn, this witch is more dangerous than the rest. She is probably the oldest of the witches we have hunted and we know based on what she has done in the past that she can be witty and deceptive."

"I've heard all this before," I say.

"Remember to play to her fetish of..." Siyo hesitates before finishing his thought, not knowing how to finish the sentence and still sound professional.

I help him. "Buttocks. I know. I've been aerobicizing mine the last two months, getting ready for this encounter. Don't worry, I know how to use my body to make sure she leads me back to her cabin. Once we know where her cabin is, we can destroy her like the others."

"It has been impossible to find out where she lives. It would be the mother lode if we can locate her hut. Remember to keep your cell phone on so we can continue to track you, Detective Jenn. Don't do anything that will put your life in danger."

"I can handle her. I've done this before, and I'll do this again. We'll get her. Just get to her cabin as soon as you get my text."

"Jenn, we've located someone in the area. It's probably her. Over and out and good luck."

"Over and out." I end the call and slide my iPhone into my front jean pocket.

I sense someone is quickly approaching. If I hadn't done this many times before I might be nervous. Why did I still feel nervous? Maybe because this particular witch is the leader of them all. I would get a major bonus if we bag her.

She is getting closer and closer, and now probably spying on me.

I am pretending to have come to this serene place to do yoga and meditation. I stretch up into an angry cat position. I do it slowly and deliberately, sticking my butt up and out and probably right in her direction. I keep it there for a count of twenty, then bring my body down and do it again. I have dealt with witches before and know how to cater to their fetishes. I do about five angry cats before I hear a raspy voice behind me. "Beautiful view."

I spin around and sit up on the rock, and feign surprise. Her voice has a foreign accent I cannot place.

I take in the witch. She is trim with piercing green eyes, and looks to be about sixty-five, but I know from my research she is about ten times that age.

"Yes, indeed a beautiful view" she repeats. I know she is referring to my angry cat pose and not the serene lake.

"Great spot for some meditation."

"Are you here all by yourself, my pretty darling?"

I hate being called *darling*. "Yes, I love finding quiet places like this to unwind."

"Good, good," she says. "Don't let me stop you. I know how important it is to stretch. Please continue with your moves. I won't disturb you."

"Thank you." I continue my rehearsed yoga routine. She is standing right next to me during my whole set of exercises. How can she expect me to concentrate when she is about a foot away, admiring me? Worse yet, when I do a position like a downward dog, she walks behind me, gaping at my butt. I continue to stretch my body to the limits while she walks around the rock to inspect me, absorbing all of my curves. I do a few extras downward dogs just for her. I feed her fetish.

"Would you like a massage?" she asks.

I turn to face her and I see she is one step away from foaming at the corners of her mouth after my yoga routine. So far, so good.

"If it's not too much trouble, I could definitely use one."

Immediately she starts rubbing my shoulders. "Oh, you are so tight, even after those wonderful yoga moves."

I can feel warmth from her hands through my spandex shirt. "That feels so good. You definitely have a way with your hands."

"Yes, I do have a way with my hands, I do."

She stops massaging me for a moment. I wonder what she is up to.

I did not have to wonder too long, however, as I feel both of her hands slide under my jeans and panties. Her palms and thin long fingers at first feel icy against the skin on my backside.

This witch knows what she wants and is not afraid to go for it. My backside is her bounty for her boldness and twisted sense of entitlement.

She removes her hands and coats them with oil, and then slides them back in under my jeans and panties. Her palms and fingers start caressing my skin. I pretend this massage is the best in the world, and in reality, it does feel indulging. She has strong hands and is able to kneed my soft skin and work it as a baker would work dough. I would lie if I said it did not feel sensual to me.

"That feels great," I tell her.

"I hope you don't mind," she says. "I know a woman may feel a little uncomfortable with a stranger touching her, especially her bottom, but I must say, you have a pair of delightful cheeks. It is quite impressive how these curves simply defy gravity." I feel a light squeeze, her way of indicating the part of my butt that defies gravity. "I also quite adore how these curves finish up down here so gracefully." I feel a tighter squeeze, this time with both hands, on my southern section.

"Oh, I hope you don't mind me using the oil, too. This is my own recipe, and it is the best massage oil out there."

"Now how does that feel?" she asks after a few minutes of massaging oil over every square inch of my ass.

"Great," I say. But there is more to her question. That oil is not massage oil, and I should have picked up on that sooner. My backside is starting to itch. First it starts itching just a little bit, like a bug bite kind of itch, but then it spreads over my whole backside to the point where I stand up and my butt feels like I sat in poison ivy.

I don't know what she put on me, but I should have known she would be sneaky. Maybe I can kill her right here. I am moving up and down on my toes.

"What's wrong?" she asks innocently.

I'll tell you what's wrong, you old witch — you just poisoned me with something. But I didn't say this, I just thought it. Instead I say, "It's strange, Ma'am, but it appears that my backside is itchy after that massage."

Itchy is an understatement. It feels like my ass is on fire. It is getting worse and worse.

"Oh dear, I might have used something else and not the massage oil. I can fix all of this though. Have you ever ridden on a broom?"

I am almost having trouble thinking as the itching is all consuming. The more I put my hands on the back of my jeans, the greater the itch. I am still able to think enough to know that my goal is to get to her cabin. A broom ride? I have never been on a broom before, and it does sound like the fastest way to get to her cabin. This witch does not know that I know she is a witch though, so I ask, "Are you a witch, Ma'am?"

"Some people call us that. We are just people of the forest, have been that way for many years. Come, let me help you. I have something back at my cabin that will take the pain instantly away."

"That sounds like a good plan to me. Thanks for your help." I can't wait for this one to go down.

She picks up a broom from behind a nearby tree and tells me to stand still. "I have to weigh you first to make sure we both can ride the broom." She palms my crotch, her thumb pressed against my sex and her long fingers flat against the part of my butt she adored. With no effort she raises me up on my tippy toes. I gasp trying to keep my balance. This old lady is strong. "123 pounds, that should work fine." So much for scales. She releases me.

"There is just one rule for riding my broom. You cannot touch it with your hands. Don't worry, I will support you, and you will be fine. It is a short trip. Ready for a fun ride?"

The itchy pain is incredible. I don't even want to think how red the skin is on my backside. Maybe I don't even have skin there anymore it hurts so much. Without waiting for me to answer her question, she pushes the broom up between my legs and says, "Keep your hands on your head and do not remove them until we land."

She sits on the back of the broom and me on the front in this weird position. How come she gets to sit sidesaddle on the broom, and I have it right between my legs? I start to ask her this when we lift off. When my feet leave the ground, I am about to tip to the side, when she grabs me not by my waist, which I would have expected, but instead cups her hands over my breasts to balance me on the broomstick! A boob fetish, too?

We are about forty feet above the ground and navigating between large trees and over the tops of small trees. The wooden broom seems to have a mind of its own and is busy rubbing back and forth against my sex, tightening my body with every rub.

I would enjoy this ride if it weren't for my ass on fire, some old hag feeling me up, and a broom whose sole objective is to give me an orgasm.

I eventually do get a massive orgasm. Actually because the broom doesn't stop moving, I get three orgasms before we touch on the ground next to her cabin. I know her fondling of my breasts triggered at least one of these orgasms.

As soon as my feet are safely on the ground, I jump off and start rubbing my backside, hoping that would help, but foolish me, it just feels worse.

"Dear, dear," she continues again.

I'd love to shove that *dear, dear* right down her throat.

She takes my wrist and walks with me to her front door, and we enter. There are no windows and just a few lit candles, which cast light on what looks and smells like garbage and decaying plants. These smells mingle with earth and incense. The witch props up her broom in the corner.

"You best now take all of your clothes off, dear, and I'll look for that lotion."

"Why do I have to take all of my clothes off?"

"Because, honey, the lotion is staining. I would hate to get stains on your pretty exercise outfit."

This made about as much sense to me as anything else today. I pull down my pants and my phone falls to the floor. Luckily, looking for the lotion distracted the witch and the earth floor meant my phone dropping did not make a sound. I am glad she didn't have a tile floor. I quickly pick up the phone and text Siyo that I am in the shack. At least I will be rescued soon, and this witch will be put down.

"Oh, here it is," she says, coming back to me. She is holding an old bottle with a cork containing white lotion. "I'll just rub this on that fine fanny of yours, and you'll be on your way."

I am totally naked facing her. I cannot believe she got me to take off all of my clothes. She is good.

"Oh, your backside is so, so red. I am so, so sorry. I'll rub it right on and you will be fine. But first..."

What does she mean "But first"? *Put that shit on my ass quickly*, I think, but playing the part, I instead ask, "Can you please put it on now?"

"First, you need to make love to my son. I have a son who has never been with a woman. I know based on your beauty that men have had the pleasure of your body."

Did she just call me a slut? The witch continues, "He is lying down on his bed in the next room. He is waiting for you. After you satisfy him, I will rub this on your backside and you will feel better."

This is insane, but what about today has been sane? I have used my body in many ways to get witches in the past. I am okay with having sex with someone to catch a witch, but having sex just to get this damn itch to stop? "Sure, I'll do it," I say. "I remember my first time. Let me show him how it's done."

The witch clasps her hands together in almost a prayer position and says, "Bless you, child." She leads me to a bed where a boy, probably about seventeen, is laying naked. He stands up when we enter, and ogles me up and down.

"She is perfect, Mama. Oh, thank you so much, I can't wait. She looks delicious."

Delicious? This should be quick. A couple of thrusts, and he'll be done.

Just by seeing me, I can tell he is excited and ready. He lies back down on his bed and commands "I want you on top of me." He is confident for a virgin. I like that and listen to him. He puts a hand on each of my butt cheeks, and I cringe with the pain of him touching my fiery backside. He then positions me over himself and pushes me down on top of him.

"That's it," he says and starts moving himself in and out of me by pulling me up by my butt and then pushing me down by it. It is painful but I know a virgin will release soon.

After fifteen minutes, he is still going strong. The same movements. I can tell by his expressions and sounds he is getting the most out of every thrust. As the minutes pass, his grip on my bottom has been tightening, and there are tears forming in my eyes from the sharp pain.

I turn to the side and realize the witch has been watching us the whole time.

"Move her butt a little bit higher when you bring her up, son" she instructs.

I feel him do this. He raises my backside a little higher and pushes me down into him with more force. He is doing this at a fast rate, giving me a better butt exercise than I could ever hope to get at the gym. Not only do I get a great butt workout, but he gets to impress his mom.

After going for over 20 minutes, while sweat is dripping off of me all over him and his bed, he explodes inside of me, like a fire hydrant. It is a big mess, and afterward he stops moving and lies back down and says, "Thank you, Mama."

Thank you, Mama? What about thank you, Jenn? I did the work. That ride broke the record and I know I'm going to be sore tomorrow.

The witch claps with delight.

I am still mounted on top of him. He then reaches up and pulls me to him. My head is resting on his chest. He keeps his slowly retracting shaft inside of me. I try to push up, but he is holding me.

"That's it," the witch says. "You hold her, and I'll rub this cream on her."

We are both sweaty, and he is rubbing my hair. Sweat is dripping off my forehead onto his chest.

I am exhausted.

I hear the sound of lotion plopping out onto a hand and feel the witch rubbing the cooling lotion on my boiling butt. It feels so good I could cry. In fact, I am pretty sure tears are rolling down my face.

She does a thorough job of covering every part of my bottom, using her dough-kneading technique. It feels so good.

The front door opens and Siyo rushes in. The witch and her son look surprised.

"Sorry, sister," I say, "your time is up." The witch steps back. I try to get myself free from lover boy, but he does not let me go.

Siyo grins first at the witch and then at me and the witch's son, still locked in a close naked embrace. I am expecting him to melt the witch by throwing water on her or something, and also to smite this young boy for having sex with me. The young lover is still holding me tightly refusing to let me go.

"Well, as long as you are giving rides to everyone, let me get a turn, too," Siyo says to me while undressing. He then adds, "You are mine and will have sex with me now."

I am shocked at his response and pry free from lover boy. I stand up and the witch takes a few more steps back. I am completely naked but not intimidated by Siyo, the witch, or her son.

Siyo is now also completely naked and pulls me close, his arm around my waist. "Now kiss me."

"You don't tell me what to do," I tell him and ignore his command. His mouth opens slightly, obviously not expecting me to talk back to him.

He nods at the witch. The witch comes from behind me, and I feel her now-familiar hands rub more of that itchy massage oil on my backside. As soon as I feel her touch, I try to move away, but Siyo is holding me tight. I feel the itching start again.

"You are an asshole because you listen more to your dick than to your heart," I tell him, squinting from my fiery itchiness.

"Do you want me to ask her to cover your whole body with that oil?" Siyo asks while grinning. "Kiss me," he instructs me again. This time I kiss him.

"Kiss me with your tongue." This time, I didn't hesitate as I feel the itching becoming overpowering again on my backside.

"Now, let's see how you ride, cowgirl. Witch, whenever she slows down, slap some more of that oil on her ass."

Siyo lets go of me and lies down on the bed. As soon as he lets go, however, instead of me mounting him and letting him have his way with me, I run to lover boy and give him a big tight hug. I whisper in his ear, "Get rid of this loser, and I'll make love to you again." I take one of his hands and place it on my breast. We are both nude, and I feel his excitement mounting, his erect shaft up against my belly.

The witch is still holding the bottle of itchy massage oil. The young boy gently lets go of me and within the span of seconds, grabs the bottle from his mom and rushes to Siyo, pouring it all over his erection.

Siyo jumps off the bed with a look of shock. Obviously, he expected to fuck me. "What the...?" Siyo yells, his very red yet still erect shaft becoming more and more inflamed. Without hesitating, he rushes for the door, not even thinking about putting back on his clothes. The door opens and closes and his screams trail off as he no doubt is running to the lake to wash off that oil.

I laughed, the witch cackled, and lover boy smiled, stretching his arms for a hug. I give lover boy a long warm embrace, and while he hugs me back, the witch rubs some of the lotion on my backside to remove the itchiness.

"He didn't ask me for the lotion," the witch tells me as she kneads my cheeks once again. "And I didn't give it to him. I enjoyed watching you with my son and would like to see him ride you again."

"I'm ready, too," lover boy says, his hand cupping one of my breasts in our embrace.

"You earned me and I am yours," I tell him. "What position would you like me in?"

"I don't know. Can you surprise me?"

I think for a minute. "I know a position both you and your mom will love." I get on the bed and do one of my favorite yoga positions, the downward dog. I glance at him and can tell this position excites him.

"Aren't you coming in?" I ask in a seductive voice.

Lover boy rushes with the same speed that he dosed Siyo and comes behind me. I know he is still new in the ways of love so when he gets close enough, I grab his shaft and line it up with me.

He pushes in, maybe a little too fast, but I do not complain. I am so glad Siyo has been punished. He starts moving at first slow, grabbing my breasts tightly. His movements start increasing. I notice the witch sitting beside us, critiquing. "You can go faster than that," she encourages her son.

I feel the rate of slaps against my backside increase, and I know "doggie-style" definitely is his favorite position of the two we tried, as I feel him release within minutes.

I woke up. I didn't expect that type of dream. I did feel empowered and in control by the end of that dream, but why did Siyo play the bad guy? Did he expect to sleep with me at the end of that dream, after being so cruel? He did seem surprised by the change of events. I grabbed my phone and texted him.

Me: Siyo, you up?

Siyo: Yep.

Than quiet for a few minutes.

Siyo: Sorry about that dream. I don't know what happened at the end. I think I got so angry when I saw you with that boy.

Me: I know, you did not seem like yourself. You seemed more like an animal.

Quiet for a few minutes.

Siyo: If you felt any degree like that when you saw me and Amy come in, I'm sorry.

Quiet for a few minutes.

Me:	Forgiven, but don't let it happen again. There's a difference between screwing up in real life and getting screwed in a dream. Okay?
Siyo:	Okay. Still on for prom Thurs?
Me:	Yes.

Heavenly Honey

You are what you eat, and I consume incredible amounts of honey, which I know definitely adds to my sweetness. What you may not know is that honey contains boron, which helps regulate estrogen and testosterone levels and provides a natural energy boost.

I use lots of honey when I make granola.

Preheat the oven to 300 degrees. Combine two cups of chopped nuts (almonds are a great choice, as we know their smell arouses passion in females), three cups of oats, ½ cup chopped dates (raisins and chopped apricots work well too), and one cup of coconut flakes in a large bowl.

Then put ½ a cup of coconut oil, one cup honey, ½ cup of brown sugar, and ¼ cup butter in the microwave for 30 seconds, and mix until all of the brown sugar dissolves. Pour this liquid into the large bowl and stir well. Then spread the granola on a baking sheet and bake for 30 minutes. Let sit at least 20 minutes before eating with milk like cereal or eat plain as a pre-foreplay treat. Yum!

Lust or Love?

Boy gets out of car. Boy nervously walks to front door holding a corsage. Girl waits at door with parents. Boy gives girl corsage. Parents assess and approve of situation. Boy and girl leave for prom.

I could tell that Siyo felt uncomfortable wearing a tux, as he ran a finger along the back collar of his shirt. He probably would have liked to show up wearing jeans and a T-shirt. He gave a small tight smile as he approached the front door with me there and my parents standing behind me.

I wore a black short dress with tights and heels. I wore my hair down and although I avoid makeup, I did make an exception and put on eye liner and lipstick.

"You look even prettier than usual," he said, making me blush.

"That's a nice tux, too."

"It has to go back tomorrow by noon, and I am responsible for any food stains on it when I return it." He let out a short laugh.

My parents asked him what time we would be back, and he hesitated for a moment. "We should be back by eleven. Is that a good time? We can come back earlier if you like." His nervousness showed by his short responses and higher than usual voice.

My parents said that would be fine, and Siyo escorted me to his car.

Our prom took place at a bar and dance club on the Seaside boardwalk. Friends came over to us when we entered and as we talked loud over the music you could feel the energy in the room. We were all excited as we had looked forward to this evening for a long time.

After a few minutes of yelling conversations over the music, I grabbed Siyo's hand and said, "Let's see some moves," while leading him to the dance floor.

Siyo can dance. I could picture him in a previous life, or maybe his grandfather, dancing around a fire chanting an Indian song. He had that same rhythm on the dance floor. After shaking everything to the music for close to an hour, we took a breather.

"I'm thirsty."

"I'll be back with some drinks," Siyo said. He walked to the bar and detoured on the way to talk with two of his friends. I could hear bits and pieces of the conversation. I overhead the words "smoking" and "Jenn" together and knew that they were talking about me. I also saw one of his friends show Siyo the metal tab from a soda can. Strange.

I could imagine as I looked around the shiny wood bar and multiple flat screen TVs that many adults hang out here on Friday and Saturday nights, downing beers and watching baseball or football. But a Thursday night with all of us underage means only sodas and Shirley Temples will be served.

Siyo returned with two cans of soda, and he opened both cans by pulling up the metal tabs. He gave me my open soda and took a sip from his. Then he pulled the tab on his can back and forth several times until it snapped off.

"You know what this is?" he asked me, holding up his tab for me to see.

"A recyclable?"

"A fuck me tab," he said, smiling, and handed it to me.

"Come again?"

"This one is yours," he continued. "Anytime you crave sex with me, just present that tab and I will deliver. Now this one," he pulled off the metal tab on my can, "is mine. When I want your sex, I will present it to you. Pretty cool, huh?" He put the tab from my can in his tux jacket pocket.

"Can I trade my tab in for something similar to what that monkey did to me in that retro sci-fi dream?" I asked him.

"Of course."

"Can I trade in my tab for a romantic dream?"

"Yes, that would be fair."

"What if I accidently drop my tab on the floor and one of your friends pick it up? Would I have to sleep with him?" I can be a tease.

He didn't laugh. "No, your tab only works for me."

"What if the tab is all bent when I trade it in for sex? Will you get angry and be naughtier to me?" I gave him a sexy childish look.

"I won't get angry, but being naughtier is not out of the question."

"Can I save up my tabs and trade them all in at once for something extra-special?"

He grit his teeth. "I know this song, let's dance." He pulled me out on the dance floor. Along with our friends, we laughed and danced for hours.

The alarm on Siyo's watch sounded at ten. "Time to start making our way back. I promised to have you back by eleven. Don't want you to turn into a pumpkin."

"We still have a whole hour before I have to be home. Let's keep dancing." I liked this song.

"No, let's go. I'd rather walk for a few minutes on the boardwalk than dance anymore."

We exited the back doors of the bar, which put us right on the Seaside boardwalk. Going from the noisy bar to the quiet boardwalk jostled my senses.

The ocean waves crashed in tune with the sounds of my heels and Siyo's shoes against the wood boardwalk. The cloudless night sky filled with stars added to nature's beauty. The air smelled of salt and amore.

I imagine watching a movie of this scene. Soft romantic music would play in the background as the hero and heroine take their relationship to the next level.

The ocean and beach, the smell of the boardwalk, the quietness magnified by the closed shops and arcades, holding hands with Siyo. Could this be love? Or the start of love? Maybe we'd crossed the line from lust to love, and how special that it occurred on the evening of our prom.

Siyo interrupted my thoughts. "I want mine now."

"Excuse me?" I asked.

Siyo reached into his tux jacket pocket and presented me with his metal tab.

"Jenn, remember our deal? Take this tab." He put the tab into my hand that he had held. "You look so hot. I want your sex now."

Obviously Siyo did not feel the same romantic feeling I felt. Or maybe he didn't distinguish romance from lust. Maybe all guys were like this.

"No one is around. Let's go under the boardwalk and fool around. I will still get you home before eleven. A great ending to a great night."

How can two people walk so closely next to each other and experience the same sounds and smells and think so different? I felt nauseous as Siyo's shallow desires erased any romantic feelings I had felt.

I did however, want this to be a special night for Siyo. There is a reason his name means "flute" and not "sensitive" or "caring". He thought with his dick.

"I don't want to get sand all over me. My parents will wonder..."

"You can go on top," Siyo interrupted.

"You are so courteous, and you are always thinking of me," I said sarcastically. I tried to think of the last time he thought of me. Nothing came to mind.

He didn't pick up on my sarcasm, or didn't seem to care. "I know, you are one lucky girl. Now come on, I want to give you a ride."

I walked behind him down the set of steps that went down to the beach. We took our shoes off. The sand felt cold against my feet, even with my tights acting as insulator. "The sand feels like snow."

"I'll warm you up," Siyo replied and French kissed me.

When he released my tongue I continued. "I don't know if we should do this. My parents are expecting us back at eleven."

"It's only a little after ten. Even if we spend twenty minutes here, I can still have you back at least fifteen minutes early."

I nodded, and he pulled me close and French kissed me again.

"You look so hot tonight. All of my friends think you are smoking too. But they can't do what I am about to do now."

I heard his zipper and the sound of his pants being pulled down, followed by the sound of a condom wrapper opening. How did he know to bring a condom to the prom?

"Only I can see you naked. Only I can do this." He took his underwear off too and put it on top of his pants in the sand.

"Here, let me help you," Siyo said. While kissing me, he pulled down my tights and undies about a quarter of the way off my body. "You don't even have to take your clothes off all of the way. They won't get sandy this way."

"Thanks for being so considerate," I said, hoping he would at least acknowledge my sarcasm. He didn't.

Siyo then laid down flat in the cold sand. "Come lay on top of me. You won't even get sand on you. Trust me."

I stretched out on top of him, every part of my body on top of his, above the sand except for the ends of my long hair. Siyo fumbled a few moments before putting himself inside of me, probably due to my tights and undies pulled only slightly down. He moved his hands to the backs of my legs above my tights and started lifting me and pulling me toward him. The movements were only slight, but it had the effect he desired.

We kept kissing each other as he moved me up and down. My hands slipped off of him several times into the cool sand. My hair veiled his face. The slow movement in and out seemed to be in synch to the sound of the distant waves.

"Oh no, oh no, oh no," he said, and I moved myself up and down to increase his ecstasy and to make this over quick so we could get out of here.

"Too quick," he added and then kissed me lightly.

"All done? Let's get out of here. It's kind of creepy under the boardwalk at night."

"Are you sure you don't want to cash in your tab for something now, too?" Siyo made a monkey sound.

"I am not comfortable under here."

We quickly got dressed and shook off the sand. I brushed my hair with my hands, trying to get out as much of the sand as possible. I didn't want my parents to see any trace of sand.

When we got up to the boardwalk, he said, "You definitely earned that tab."

"Gee, thanks," I replied. "Any more sand in my hair?"

He brushed my hair with his hands. "I don't see any."

I brushed some sand off of him.

"Did you find that great?" Siyo asked me, but I could tell by his tone that he told me more than asked me what I truly thought. I didn't respond and so he continued, "What an awesome ending to an awesome night. Wait till I tell the guys. I wonder if they scored, too…"

We held hands and walked off the beach without any more conversation, back up to the boardwalk and then to his car. When we got to his car, I asked, "Can I cash in my tab for a good dream tonight? Something romantic?"

"Sure thing, Jenn. I just happen to have that dream snatcher in my car." He winked at me. I bet he never goes anywhere without it. I didn't know why I asked for a dream. Maybe because I felt I needed something romantic tonight. I started wondering if Siyo's grandmother felt similarly when Siyo interrupted my thoughts. "Here it is. Okay, where is your tab?"

I handed him my tab, and he cut my finger. My bleeding finger didn't seem to faze him one bit. He didn't have a Band-Aid for me, so I just sucked my finger until it stopped.

"Make it something to do with the boardwalk."

"What?" He must have been thinking about something else, probably about telling his friends that the fuck me tab worked like a charm.

"Make my dream something to do with the boardwalk. I always find the boardwalk full of mystique."

"Sure thing, Jenn."

He had me home a few minutes before eleven. My parents were both dressed in their pajamas when they met us at the door.

"Did you kids have a good time?" my mom asked.

"We had fun but the music played too loud," Siyo replied. I didn't speak so he kept talking. "We danced the entire time, and then I rushed back to get her home by eleven. Definitely a memorable night." He paused. "I am so *into* your daughter."

My mom and dad smiled, and I knew this last sentence gained him extra points with my parents. I also knew by him stressing the word *into* he definitely implied something else. Something inappropriate. He'd actually told my parents that he had fucked me and got completely away with telling them. I turned away slightly.

I hoped they didn't notice any stray pieces of sand on his clothing. My parents liked and trusted Siyo. They didn't know what he did to me though. When I got undressed that night, I found the metal tab I had earned, and put it in my nightstand drawer. I hoped I'd spent my metal tab wisely.

I am holding hands with Siyo while we walk on the Seaside boardwalk. It is a beautiful day, already late afternoon and the sun has started making its way toward the horizon, getting closer and closer to disappearing behind the ocean. I am wearing a short casual spring dress, and my hair is blowing mildly in the ocean breeze.

We walk up to the Frog Bog stand. This is my favorite game on the boardwalk. You pay for a basket of rubber frogs, and there is a small see-saw positioned in front of you. You place a frog on one side of the see-saw, and you bang a hammer down on the other side. The frog flies through the air and if it lands in one of the moving plastic lily pads, you win a prize.

Siyo and I are laughing and having lots of fun. All of our frogs have missed the lily pads, and we have just one left that I launch high in the air and then the frog lands smack center on the lily pad. I win a prize!

There are lots of prizes to choose from, including a large puppet hanging up in front of me. It is one of those ventriloquist puppets seen on comedy stages years ago. You know the one, where the guy is drinking water while the puppet is talking. This puppet is wearing a gray suit and has a silly look on its face.

"I want that puppet!" I say with excitement. The game attendant unfastens the puppet and hands it to me.

We continue walking, and I am holding the puppet with one hand and Siyo is holding my other hand. The puppet's head is resting on my shoulder and the puppet's body is snug against my bosom. "I guess this is what it feels like to hold a baby," I say and Siyo grins.

We play a few more games and eat dinner and then he drops me off at my house. I kiss him goodbye on his cheek.

The entranceway is dark, and I do not want to wake up my parents. I follow the usual routine of tiptoeing into the kitchen, getting a glass of water, and retiring to my bedroom. I find it a challenge to complete these steps while holding the puppet.

I close the door to my bedroom and put the light on. I am not sure what I am going to do with this puppet but I enjoyed winning it. Maybe I can try that trick I saw on TV years before. I sit on my bed and place the puppet on my lap. Then I take my glass of water and try talking. It sounds like me talking underwater.

Then the puppet turns to face me and says in a shrilly cartoon voice, "It's a lot easier without the water, baby."

I put my glass down and in shock respond, "You can talk?"

"Sure, baby, now try this. I am going to drink this water here, and you try talking. This may work just a bit better."

I am still in shock. I don't move toward the glass.

"Oh, that's right," the puppet says, "I forget who the puppet is now."

And all of sudden he is controlling my body. I feel my hands move to the glass of water, and I pick up the glass and put it to my lips. Some water trickles down the front of my dress.

"Now look who's the dummy, baby! Oh, looks like you have a drinking problem." The puppet follows with a high-pitched laugh.

He continues to make me drink the water, or to be more precise, slowly spill the cup of water down the front of my dress. I feel cold water all over my body and legs. It keeps getting wetter and wetter as I continue to pour the rest of the glass of water down the nape of my neck instead of into my mouth.

He makes me put the empty glass back on the table.

"Now look what you've done, baby. I hope you are not too wet underneath that dress. I wouldn't want you to catch a chest cold." He is still on my lap and raises one small wooden hand and feels the front of my dress. "Oh, silly puppet. You did get yourself all wet." He then moves his hand directly over my bra and squeezes, his tiny hand big enough to completely pinch my nipple. I jump out of pain and surprise.

"Hey, no moves, baby, unless I pull the strings. You got that?"

He makes me nod my head.

"Good, now let's try that one again." He pinches my other nipple, much harder than the first time, and then twists his fingers slightly, adding greatly to the pain. I hold in the hurt and don't move.

"Baby, that's my girl. Now what can the two of us do now? Poor baby, all wet. I know, we will take these wet clothes off of you and get you nice and dry in your birthday suit. I always wanted to see what a puppet looks like without her clothes on."

He makes me stand up. His arms are resting on my shoulders, and he is hugging me as a tired child would hug a parent. His head is pressing against my bosom. Then he makes me put him down.

"Let's get this wet dress off you as quickly as we can, shall we?"

He is controlling my hands to try to get my dress off. I find my hands clumsily trying to take my dress off, but it is obvious the little puppet has never undressed a female before. The zipper is in the back but I cannot talk to this dummy to tell him this.

"Hmmm, I'll have to get creative here." He makes me lift him up, and he puts both small hands on the neck of my dress and makes me let go of him. I hear a ripping sound as his crude technique works.

My first thought is I hope that sound did not wake up my parents. But this is a crazy thought, as they can save me from this puppet. But then do I want them to see me almost naked with a wooden toy?

He slowly lands on the floor, taking my ripped dress with him.

"There, that's better, baby." He makes me walk over the pile of wet ripped clothes that used to be my fancy spring dress. I am standing just in my bra and panties.

"You truly don't need a dress anyway, baby. You look fairly decent just in your undergarments." He makes me pick him up and put him on my bed. Then he makes me sit on his little narrow wooden lap.

It feels like I am sitting on two baseball bats. He grinds his hard wooden knees back and forth against my bottom. "Baby, does that feel as good for you as it does for me?" He makes me nod.

"You chose me as your prize, baby," he says. "Now let me see my prize. There may be something in here for me. Let us see what I win."

He pulls back the front of my panties, and like a kid opening a candy bag, he puts his other hand inside. I feel a small wooden hand fumbling through my tiny hairs and with a stir, I know he has found his prize. I feel his hand move in and out. My body begins to tighten.

"Now baby, I don't want my puppet thinking any impure thoughts. Got it?" He makes me nod.

My body continues to tighten as he plays with me, and I am about to experience my first puppet-induced orgasm, when suddenly, he stops.

"Oh, so close but so far away," he says. My frustration level builds.

He makes me stand up and then sit back down again, this time on his little wooden head. I feel his mouth open and close on my tush. "Yum, yum,

yum, plenty of meat back here. I know what I'm having for dinner, and also for dessert." It feels like I am sitting on a pair of wide plastic tweezers, opening and closing.

When he gets his fill, he makes me stand up again. My hands move and pull down my panties. There is no way this dummy is going to be able to unlatch my bra. Sure enough, he makes me pick him up again and move him within arm's range of the front of my bra, and he rips it off.

"There, there, baby. Aren't you much more comfortable in your birthday suit? I finally get to see a puppet without her clothes and you do not disappoint, baby." He makes me turn around slowly several times.

"Baby's got back," he says and then makes me stand still, naked, in front of him. He does not touch me or control my body, but just sits back on my bed and stares at me with his stupid puppet expression. I feel not only frustrated but also exposed. Of course I feel exposed. I am standing naked in front of a horny puppet.

Maybe it is over and the possessed puppet is no more. This is wishful thinking I realize as he makes me get on all fours in a crawling position, and then he climbs on top. He is lying on my back and his hands are fastened to my breasts. He pinches and twists my nipples and he has already trained me not to move in pain when he does this. He kicks my waist with his plastic shoes. "Giddy-up, horsy." He makes me crawl around my bedroom with him as my passenger. "Slow and steady," he says.

"Look, no hands, Mommy," he says while letting go of my nipples, his hands in the air. I am still crawling with him as my rider.

He then turns around and starts slapping my backside, alternating his little wood hands against my butt cheeks. "Baby, I know you can go faster." I start moving faster as he is slapping. He is making me bump into my bedroom furniture. This better not wake up my parents.

He makes me bump into an ironing board and the iron falls down on the carpeting. He makes me stop next to the iron.

"Hey, baby, what's this?" He picks up the iron and I notice it is plugged in. "Baby, you should never leave an iron plugged in. Baby, don't you know that not only is it a waste of electricity, but that someone can get hurt? And look, you have it set to Cotton, the hottest setting. Now don't you feel like a dummy? Baby, don't you know you can get burned?"

And with that, he presses the iron firmly against my backside and holds it there while his high pitched laugh mixes with my screams.

I woke myself up and felt furious. I picked up my phone and texted Siyo. I didn't care that it was four in the morning.

Me: What the hell?

A few minutes pass.

Siyo: Hey, just getting back to
            sleep. Take it easy. That
            dream turned me on. Good
            dream, huh?

Me: No, I did not feel in
            control. That puppet freaked
            me out.

Siyo: Did any parts of it turn u
            on?

Me: No.

A brief pause.

Me: Maybe a little. I liked
            walking with you on the
            boardwalk.

Siyo: It's give and take. I gave
            you the mushy boardwalk part
            of the dream, and I enjoyed
            what the puppet did to you.
            Don't worry. I promise I'll
            never win you a puppet like
            that.

Me: I wanted something romantic,
            not wacky.

Siyo: The first part had romance,
            right?

Me:	I guess so.
Siyo:	I'll make it up to you. Can I come over Sunday?
Me:	Yes, will text.
Siyo:	Okay. I promise a better dream Sunday night.
Me:	Okay.

I stared at the ceiling. I started thinking about Siyo's grandmother and wondered if the dreams that Siyo's grandfather created scared her and eventually led to her demise.

I don't get spooked easily, but being controlled by that horny wooden puppet came close.

It took a while, but I finally went back to sleep.

Whipped Cream War

Whipped cream is so decadent. Have you ever had a whipped cream fight with that special somebody?

How did it end? If it ends like my whipped cream fights, you would be hoping for an endless supply of whipped cream. Real homemade whipped cream tastes so much richer than store bought, and it is so easy to make!

Whip one cup of heavy cream in an electric mixer until soft peaks appear on top. Add two teaspoons of vanilla (good quality vanilla, not the one gallon size from the dollar store), and four tablespoons of sugar. Continue to whip until the soft peaks become stiff.

New Hope

The sun snuck in through the Venetian blinds, playing artist and painting zebra stripes all over my body. One more hour of sleep would be nice, but once I'm up, I'm up.

While growing up, many kids lived on my block and I couldn't wait to get up early on Saturdays and Sundays to go outside and play with friends. Now that I am 18, I wouldn't mind sleeping in a little on the weekends.

I performed a couple of yoga moves in my bed, stretching out my lower back. Saturday night shifts always leave my back a little sore on Sunday mornings.

It felt good to do an "angry cat" and stretch my lower back muscles. After a couple of other stretches, I got up and opened my bedroom door. The smell of coffee and French toast always made me smile. This smell got stronger as I walked into the kitchen. I gave my mom and dad hugs, and I took a seat at the kitchen table.

"How did work go last night?" my dad asked.

"Long. Glad it's Sunday."

"How's your paper cut?" my mom asked, noticing the new Band-Aid on my finger.

"Okay. Keeping it covered to not get infected."

My mom had a concerned look on her face but changed the subject. "Do you have your waitress uniform for me to wash?"

"Thanks, Mom. Yes, it's in the white plastic bag."

"We're taking a day trip to New Hope. Your father has been craving coffee ice cream from that homemade creamery place there, and I'm looking forward to walking along the canal. Why don't you join us?"

"I'm supposed to get together with Siyo today. Let me text him after breakfast — maybe he can come along, too."

My dad placed several slices of French toast on a plate, and my mom chopped up a pear and added it on top, and then brought it to me at the table.

"Don't forget the powdered sugar," my dad said and sprinkled sugar from a plastic container over the French toast.

I put a forkful of the French toast in my mouth. "Yum." My dad made the world's best French toast, crunchy on the outside and chewy inside.

I enjoyed every moment of being waited on, especially after many shifts of waiting on people at the diner. My mom, dad, and I made small talk and enjoyed breakfast together.

After breakfast, I texted Siyo to see if he wanted to come with us for a day trip to New Hope.

Me: Siyo, you up?

Siyo: Yes, nice out. What are we doing?

Me: Come with me and my parents to New Hope.

Siyo: Done. Time?

Me: 10 am.

Siyo: CUL8R.

I always enjoyed exploring New Hope. A tiny bridge over the Delaware River connects Lambertville in New Jersey with New Hope in Pennsylvania. Both towns were fun to explore, filled with interesting shops that sold unusual crafts, collectibles, and antiques. After several hours of shopping, we would wind down at an old-fashioned ice cream parlor in New Hope.

The doorbell rang around ten-thirty, and my mom opened the door for Siyo. Siyo shook my dad's hand and gave my mom a light peck on the cheek. Siyo also gave me a peck on the cheek.

"Haven't been to New Hope in a long time," he told us at breakfast.

"One of the best ice cream shops is right in New Hope," my dad told him.

"I've been to that place. Great atmosphere," Siyo replied.

The kitchen still smelled like breakfast, and we sat around the table and talked some more. Siyo had brought over a round coffee crumb cake, and my mom cut us all pieces with Siyo getting an extra big piece.

"Would you like something to drink, Siyo?" my mom asked.

"Yes, please. Can I have a cup of coffee? No milk, just sugar." My mom smiled and happily started preparing his coffee. I felt funny about this though. My parents could wait on me, but Siyo should get his own coffee. Not sure why I felt this. Maybe because I like my parents just to wait on me, or maybe it's confirmation that Siyo takes from everyone, not just me but also from my parents.

"Jennifer," my mom said jostling me out of my thoughts. "You are still wearing the same bathing suit you wore two years ago. Let's get you something in style for this summer at the shore. We'll go to the same shop we went to last time for your bathing suits."

"They still fit me fine though, Mom."

"Let's at least look, maybe you'll see something you like, okay?"

"Yes Mom, that would be nice, thanks. It's a fun shop to look around anyway. Lots of nautical items."

We talked for a while about some of the shops in New Hope, and the nice walk we would like to take along the canal.

"We should get going. The earlier we get there, the greater the chance we'll find a good parking spot," my dad said.

After Siyo finished his large slice of coffee cake and cup of coffee, I cleaned up the table and put the dishes and forks in the dishwasher. We took my dad's Accord with my mom and dad in the front and me and Siyo in the back. It's about a half hour's drive to New Hope.

My mom and dad talking with each other combined with the music from the radio, created a sound barrier so that Siyo and I could quietly discuss Thursday night's puppet dream without being overhead.

Taylor Swift's "Blank Space" played on the radio as Siyo began the conversation. "I know you didn't like that dream, but it stirred something deep inside of me."

"Being exploited by a horny sadistic puppet is not my idea of a romantic dream," I whispered back.

"I enjoyed watching the puppet undress you and then ride you. I know that sounds perverted."

"It doesn't sound perverted. It is perverted." My voice rose slightly above a whisper, and I decided I didn't want to risk my parents overhearing our dream conversation in the car. We talked about the summer instead.

Shortly after we passed the sign *Welcome to New Hope,* my dad said, "Keep your eyes open for a parking spot."

"There's one," Siyo said after a few blocks of us looking. Siyo found a good spot right near the ice cream shop. He definitely just earned some more points with my dad. It was rare to find a spot so close on a crowded Sunday such as today.

You could definitely feel summer around the corner, even with today's overcast and cool weather. We enjoyed walking around and window shopping and going into some of the shops to see the wares for sale. Eventually we arrived at the store that sold bathing suits.

It felt extremely awkward looking for a bathing suit with my parents and my boyfriend. Just with my parents would be okay, and probably just with Siyo would be okay, too. But all three together made me uncomfortable. Especially knowing Siyo had seen me naked on more than one occasion, but my parents did not know this.

"How about this one, sweetie?" my mom asked, holding up a conservative one-piece bathing suit with a built-in skirt around the bottom.

"Is it my size? I can try it on." I held it in my hands with two other conservative bathing suits my parents picked out.

Siyo, on the other hand, obviously thought more about the environment, as the bathing suits he picked out for me to try on had a lot less material on it than those selected by my parents.

"Try this one, Jenn," Siyo said, handing me a green string bikini with very little material on the top and bottom. Without looking too closely at it, I added it to the pile to try on.

"Thanks, Siyo, I might get seriously sunburned in something like that."

"Green is one of your colors," Siyo replied, not acknowledging that this was the third string bikini he picked out for me to try on.

My arm started getting heavy from holding all of the bathing suits. "Okay, time to try these on. You three get a seat, and I'll be right back with the ones I like best."

As my parents and Siyo sat down on low-to-the-ground red round velvet ottomans, I went into the dressing room to try on each of the bathing suits.

I decided to try on the ones my parents picked first.

I would rather wear a one-piecer than a bikini. Although I knew my body would look great in a bikini, my modesty usually won out. The first one-piecer I tried on with the built-in skirt fit me well. My mom knew my style. I went out to model it, and my mom and dad said they liked it, while Siyo stayed quiet.

After I went back in to try on the second one-piece bathing suit, I laughed a little out loud, thinking how Siyo would describe the bathing suit I just modeled for him and my parents. *"You have a kick-ass figure, Jenn, you need to be proud of it and show those curves."* He would never think of saying something like that in front of my parents though. It would be a long walk for him back from New Hope if those words ever slipped out of his mouth.

The other one-piece bathing suits I tried on weren't as flattering as the first one, so I didn't bother modeling them outside the dressing room. Then I tried on a neon red string bikini.

Did I even have it on right? I did not know for sure. I blushed even looking at myself in the mirror. Instead of taking it off right away however, I decided to model this one for the audience outside. At least it would be a good laugh and probably embarrass the heck out of Siyo.

"Is my audience ready for the next outfit the lovely and talented Jenn will be showcasing?" I broadcasted in a deep voice from inside my dressing room with a fake accent, trying to sound like a professional announcer.

"Yes."

"Okay."

"Bring it on."

I exited the dressing room in the red string bikini. As I walked toward my parents and Siyo, I felt completely nude. I quickly brushed my thumbs against my sides to make sure at least some fabric covered me. "What does everyone think of the bathing suit Siyo picked out for me to try on?" I asked the three innocently as I spun around.

My mom said immediately, "Now, Jennifer, you change out of that right now. I will not have my daughter wearing nothing but shoe laces on the Seaside beach! Besides, imagine the sunburns possible when you are frolicking under the summer sun close to naked."

My mom and dad both laughed, but Siyo said, "I think this one looks good. And it is on sale, too." His voice trailed off, feeling outvoted and being stared down by my parents. Both my mom and dad gave him looks that made his last comment on the bathing suit sound more pleading. "But it is on sale."

I giggled so hard back in the dressing room that I almost peed. Eventually I found a bikini that contained much more material, safely covering many of the curves the string bikini had revealed. I modeled this one for my parents and Siyo and everyone gave it a thumbs up. As I spun around modeling, I wondered what my parents and Siyo were thinking. My mom probably thought, *"My daughter is all grown up."* Siyo probably thought, *"I can't wait to massage suntan lotion all over her bod at the beach this summer."* My dad probably knew Siyo's impure thoughts, which would make my dad simmer.

"Okay, we got our bathing suits. Let's go for a walk along the canal but first ice cream. Dad's turning red, and I know he is looking forward to his coffee ice cream."

After ice cream and a short walk along the canal, we visited a funky costume shop around the corner from where we bought the bathing suits. Even though we were more than six months away from Halloween, we always had fun looking at costumes. We were told this costume store had a great reputation with theatre companies, who would frequently shop here for their show wardrobes.

We opened the door and bells that were tied to the door announced our arrival to the shopkeeper. As we entered, our eyes needed to adjust to the dim atmosphere. The only lights in the store were electronic candles that looked like real candles, lit everywhere for a haunting effect.

"Welcome," an old short man announced from behind the counter. "Please let me know if I can help you find anything."

Racks upon racks contained countless costumes. There were also some larger, more expensive, costumes in the back room. I found myself walking with my parents while Siyo explored the racks by himself.

When my parents and I were done browsing, we walked to the front of the store, and I noticed Siyo leaving the register, having already bought something. He held a brown bag containing his purchase protectively under his arm.

"What do you have there?" I asked Siyo.

"Just buying something for my…for my mom." He didn't make eye contact with me though, just looked at his bag. I knew he felt relieved that my parents didn't see what he had purchased.

On our way back from New Hope, we didn't talk much, as we were all tired.

Siyo slipped a metal tab into my hand in the backseat, the one I gave him for a romantic dream. "This is for my dream tonight."

I took a deep breath and closed my eyes.

Before we said goodbye, he made sure to open my cut up again with the dream snatcher.

"I am guessing this will not be a romantic dream, will it?" I asked while applying pressure to my bleeding finger.

"That costume shop triggered a great idea for a dream, and there might be some romance. You should go along with it though, knowing that your boyfriend will enjoy it immensely." Siyo grinned.

My last thought before falling asleep that night had to do with destroying that dream snatcher.

I am standing in a gothic-style entranceway dressed up for Halloween and awaiting trick-or-treaters. Creepy Halloween music is playing in the background.

There is a large ornate mirror in the corner of the room, and I walk closer to examine this antique. It is massive with lots of dragons carved on all four sides. I do not believe in dragons, but the detail in which this dark mahogany piece has been carved has me rethinking whether dragons do actually exist. They are so realistic, with large buggy eyes and spiny backs.

I see myself in the mirror. I am dressed up as a witch. I am wearing the traditional pointed black witch's hat, my long hair is down past my shoulders, and I am dressed in all black. A long-sleeved laced black blouse accompanies a short skirt with black tights and high heels. My blouse has a low-cut neckline. I could be imagining this, but my breasts look slightly bigger and more exposed in this outfit. An abundance of cleavage is showing.

My outfit is not the kind of outfit one would want to waste staying at home and dishing out candy to bratty kids. This is the kind of outfit you would like to be seen in at an upscale Halloween party to make all of the guys go gaga.

I notice a large silver platter piled high with candy by the door. I walk over and see lots of different types of candy including my favorite, M&Ms. I open a pack and start chomping on them when the doorbell rings.

I pick up the tray of candy and open the door. There is a young girl wearing a Little Red Riding Hood costume, looking up at the candy. I bend down to her level.

"Aren't you supposed to say something?" I ask while she eyes the candy.

"Trick or treat," she replies and grabs a handful of small fun-sized bags of M&Ms and puts them in the large plastic pumpkin she is carrying.

I close the door and a few moments later the bell rings again. I open the door and a little boy dressed as Darth Vader faces me.

"Trick or treat," says the muffled boy's voice through the Darth Vader mask. I lower myself to his level, holding the tray of candy below my breasts. He grabs a bag of Skittles and then also a couple of Milky Way bars. He puts lots of candy in his pillow sack, which is already heavy with Halloween goodies. Each piece of candy he takes puts his tiny hands closer to my breasts.

"That's enough for you," I say. "Save some for the other kids, greedy Vader."

Mini Darth Vader draws his large red light saber. "Nobody talks to me like that." He starts swinging his saber about his head. I had to duck.

"Hey, watch it, Vader-want-to-be. You can hurt someone or break something." I am not sure if I should take him seriously or laugh.

This only made Mini Darth Vader angrier. He then takes his life saber and tries to stab me with it. This kid is crazy. Luckily because of his height, I spread my legs and the life saber misses me and he stabs the air right around the height of my knees.

He keeps the saber there for a moment, and then pushes it straight up as hard as he can, the saber stopping against my sex. I could feel his strength as he pushes it up enough to raise me on my tippy toes.

"Darth Vader rules all," he says. "Even witches."

"Hey, stop that," I say.

He did not stop. In fact, he starts rubbing the saber back and forth, as if trying to start a fire there. He is probably a Boy Scout, and just like a Boy Scout might try rubbing sticks together to make a fire, he is making his own fire between my legs.

He continues rubbing and my hands are holding the tray of candy so I cannot push him away without dropping everything on the floor. Plus, it feels pleasing – to the point where my body starts tightening.

"Trick or treat?" the little Darth Vader asks me.

I didn't respond, too wrapped up in my own sensual feelings.

He stops rubbing.

"Hey!" I say.

"Trick or treat?" the little Darth Vader asks me again.

"Definitely treat," I say, gritting my teeth and he nods and continues rubbing again.

The orgasm is one step away from mind-blowing. I almost drop the tray of candy on the floor in response.

He puts his saber away and bows in front of me.

"You are..." I am trying to think of the right word... "quite skillful, Darth Vader. You definitely deserve all of this candy. Open that pillow case."

I empty the entire tray of candy into his pillow case.

I close the door and get ready to turn off the lights, as I have no more sweets to give out.

Before I turn off the switch though, the doorbell rings again. I open the door and in front of me is a man dressed up as Dracula. He is tall with a wrinkly face, and I can see his sharp fangs as he smiles at me. He is wearing a long black cape.

"Trick or treating is for kids not adults, Mister," I say.

A raspy "Trick or treat" is his only response.

Absentmindedly, I pick up the tray and tell him to take his pick of sweets.

He is staring down at the tray.

"What?" I say and then look down to see what he is looking at.

The tray is empty. I forgot I gave Darth Vader all my candy, so I am holding up an empty tray to Dracula. Worse though, I am holding the tray right under my breasts. My breasts are resting on the tray. The amount of cleavage showing isn't making the situation any less awkward.

Before I can lower the tray, he says, "I'm not sure which treat I want. Can I take both?"

I am about to say something when he stretches out his long thin arms from under his cape and grabs my boobs, one in each hand, and squeezes.

"Hey, what do you think you're doing?" I say.

"I am only taking what you offered me, young
lady. You offered me sweets, and both of these
indeed look very sweet."

I drop the tray on the floor and put my hands over
his to unclamp them from my chest.

His hands remain where they are. In fact, he
squeezes harder.

"Hey, you can't get away with this," I say while
trying to remove his long boney fingers from my
breasts.

Then he pulls me closer to him, by my breasts of course, and leans over. I think he is going to whisper something in my ear, but instead I feel a bite on my neck.

"Fuck," I yell.

"Yes, yes, all in good time. You are tasty." There is some blood around his lips, and I watch him lick his lips. "Yes, very tasty. How do you feel?"

I feel a trickle of warm liquid go down my neck, and I know it is blood.

"I feel like kicking you between your legs. What do you want from me?"

"That's simple. You."

And with that, he releases his hands, zooms behind me, lifts up my skirt, and digs his sharp fangs into the soft skin of my bottom, piercing me right above my legs. His teeth sink deep into me, right through my tights and panties.

"Stop," I say but he ignores me and drinks generously from me. He indulges for several minutes, sounding like someone sucking a combination of air and water through a straw.

When he releases, I feel light-headed. I wonder how much of my blood he drank.

He zooms to my front again. His pale face is flushed and again he licks his lips. "You are so delicious. I want more. Lots more. But first you did say 'fuck' I believe, and I will oblige."

He hoists me up on his shoulder. He does this with the same amount of effort a school child would use to throw a backpack over his shoulder. I am his backpack. I am balanced on his shoulder with his hand on my backside.

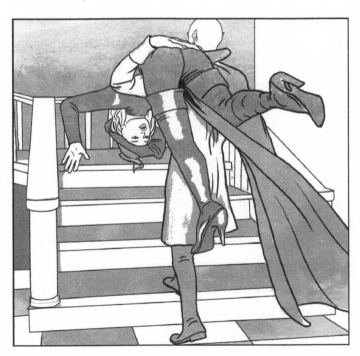

He walks up a staircase and my first thought to wriggle free is probably not a wise idea. I do not want to fall down a flight of steps. I also do not want to make this blood sucker angry.

He opens a door at the top of the stairs and callously plops me down on a bed.

I am on my back on blood red silk sheets.

"Not only do you have the honor to lie on Dracula's bed," he says, "you have the honor to receive Dracula."

He claps his hands and two short women appear. They look like twins. They are wearing black suits and have shaved heads and pure white skin. I am guessing they are vampires too.

"My lord," they say in unison.

"Prepare her," he commands.

"Yes, my lord," they say again in unison.

The twins rapidly undress me. Their faces show no expressions as they do their work. My shoes, tights, dress, bra, undies – even my hat is taken off. I am completely naked within seconds.

I glance at Dracula and he is now naked as well. Dracula's body reminds me of an emaciated senior citizen.

"How would you like her?" one of the twins asks.

It is quiet for a moment. "Turn her over."

The other twin flips me on my belly like a burger on a grill.

"Yes, that will do fine."

One of the twins ties my wrists to the bed post. Judging by the sounds I hear behind me, I am guessing the other twin is going down on Dracula.

The twin working with me then closes two of her fingers on one of my nipples and pushes a finger from her other hand into my sex and starts playing with me.

I know this is all part of what Dracula wants. Prepare me so I will be ready to have sex with him. I try to focus my mind on food or school or work or my family, but it is hard to ignore the pleasures induced by this vampire girl. I make no sounds but she knows I have just climaxed. "She is all yours," she tells Dracula.

"Leave us," Dracula tells the twins, and they both vanish.

I feel him climb on top of me with his erect shaft against my butt. He bites my neck and while sucking plunges his shaft deep inside of me. One of his hands is balancing his body on top of me. His other hand reaches across my breasts, with his arm pressing into one breast and his hand squeezing the other.

He moves in and out almost like a machine, each deep thrust feels like the thrust before. He might look like an emaciated senior citizen, but he has the endurance of a marathon runner.

He stops sucking and focuses completely on the pleasures he feels going in and out of me.

He grabs my hair and pulls my head back slightly, his thrusting increasing at a steady rate.

Without making a sound, Dracula explodes inside of me, still maintaining his thrusting rate for a few more pushes before resting on top of me.

"You are delicious," he whispers in my ear. "I hope you are satisfied now, young lady. I did as you requested. But now, you owe me."

I feel a sharp pain on my bottom, as once again his fangs sink into my soft skin, like a fork into butter.

The pain caused me to scream slightly and I woke myself up. I felt used and drained. Drained probably because of the large amount of imaginary blood I lost. I laid on my bed and stared up at the ceiling, thinking about my previous dreams. The dreams had been getting darker and darker, and my hope for romantic adventures had been replaced by fear of what Siyo might do to me in my dreams. I kept thinking back to Siyo's grandmother and wondered if she felt as I do now. Siyo and I did not have a healthy relationship.

I knew a bit about psychology. What Siyo had acted out in his dreams, or to be more precise, what he had his characters act out in his dreams, revealed his perverted nature and selfishness. I don't think all boys think this way. If they did, I could imagine the word "love" would be completely removed from the dictionary, or have phrases like "See lust" or "See horny puppet" appear after it.

Crunchy Pumpkin Seeds

Pumpkin seeds are such a sensual snack. They can arouse you and your partner, as they are high in magnesium which raises testosterone levels. Pumpkin seeds also contain omega-3, which keeps sex hormone production at its peak!

Preheat the oven to 400 degrees. Melt together four tablespoons olive oil, four tablespoons honey, ½ teaspoon ground ginger, and a ½ teaspoon nutmeg. Add this mixture to three cups raw pumpkin seeds and mix well. Spread out evenly on a greased baking pan and bake for fifteen minutes. Let cool before eating.

Hello, Goodbye

The following Sunday, I had a morning shift at the diner, and so agreed to meet Siyo for lunch at his place afterward.

Rain started during my drive to the diner. I pulled in and parked where the employees park in the back. The pouring rain made it feel like I was in the middle of a car wash. I could barely see through the windshield. I didn't have an umbrella, so I walked as quickly as I could without risking slipping in my heels. My clothes felt soaked when I entered and I knew the diner would be crowded. Diners are usually busier on rainy days. I like busy. Busy means more tips.

Toward the end of my shift, a tall guy without an umbrella entered the diner from the pouring rain and asked John at the register the best way to pick up the Garden State Parkway going north toward New York.

I heard all this as I took an order for the couple in the booth closest to the register. John tried to be helpful but lacked familiarity with the highway going north as he lives south of the diner, so I jumped into the conversation to help out.

"You're lost?" I asked.

The stranger paused for a moment, looked at me and maintained eye contact, careful to keep that eye contact and not look at any other part of me.

He had bright blue eyes and a clean-shaven cute face. He reminded me of a young Mel Gibson. He wore a blue plain button-down shirt over jeans and a black jacket. He did not even wear a rain jacket. Definitely not a weatherman!

"Trying to get to the Garden State Parkway North. I don't know why New Jersey designs roads like this. It always seems easier to go south, but try to get north…it's like New Jersey doesn't want you to get back to New York. The GPS on my phone keeps sending me the wrong way, so I'm guessing some construction project completed around here within the last few weeks and my GPS doesn't know about the new on ramps."

"It's real easy from here to pick up the GSP. Make a right out of the diner, take your first jug handle, and then within two miles you should see signs for the GSP." A *jug handle* is how you make a U-turn in New Jersey and *GSP* is the Jersian's name for the Garden State Parkway.

"Got it. I appreciate that Miss…" And then he hesitated. His eyes quickly left my eyes and checked my hand to make sure I did not wear an engagement ring or wedding band. *No, I am not married. I am still in high school. I do have a boyfriend though, who I don't love yet, who loves me for my body, who is a pervert, and into kinky dreams involving witches and puppets.*

"Jenn."

"I'm Steve." He shook my hand. *What am I, going on a job interview with him?*

"Just trying to help." I turned and walked away, trying to guess where his eyes were now as I did my sassy cat walk back to the diner's kitchen.

I consider myself a confident person in general, and this confidence came across even when I had no knowledge of a particular topic. I happened to have a lousy sense of direction, and although I sounded convincing, I did not know for sure if the directions I gave him were to the New Jersey Turnpike or to the Garden State Parkway.

When I saw Steve enter the diner about twenty minutes later, I realized I sent him to the Turnpike by mistake. He looked wetter than before, and angrier too, but still cute.

I quickly served the five waters balanced on my tray to a noisy family and walked right over to him. "Steve, right?"

Steve nodded and I continued, "I might have sent you to the Turnpike instead of the Parkway."

He nodded again, his expression on the border of anger and laughter. "What gives you that idea? The Turnpike is a completely different highway than the Garden State Parkway. I drove back and forth several times before coming back here for more help. Nothing else is even open at this time on a Sunday morning."

"The good people of New Jersey like to sleep in on Sundays, or come here for breakfast. Besides," I tried defending myself, "you are to blame and are at fault. You chose to listen to me, not knowing I have a poor sense of direction. You should have first confirmed that someone knows the area before asking that person for directions."

Steve didn't respond, his mouth slightly open unsure what to say next.

From my own self-assessment, I know I do not take blame well. I would probably have made a damn good personal injury attorney. If something happened that got blamed on me, I had gotten good over the years turning it around to make someone else responsible. "Jenny," I can still hear my second grade teacher say, "I cannot believe you spilled blue paint all over the floor," to which I quickly responded, "Well, Ms. O'Brien, if the last person who used this jar had tightened the top well, this accident would never have happened." Ms. O'Brien had no response, just like Steve had no response now.

He considered what I had said. Then he burst out laughing. "Thank you for reminding me to always get a second opinion on driving directions. I just assumed if you work in a diner, you must know the local roads around the diner. Please forgive me." He continued to laugh.

He had a little boy laugh, and I tried to hold it in, but found myself giggling a little bit too.

"Okay. So how do I get back home?" He looked at me after saying this, waiting for me to say something. I allowed a few moments of awkward silence before responding.

"You can ask somebody else who has a better sense of direction than me."

"What if I like talking with you?" he asked. "What are your core skills besides geography?" He smiled an adorable smile.

"My shift ends in about fifteen minutes. If you want to know more about me, wait for my shift to end." My heart skipped a beat when I said this. *What am I doing?*

"I will do that. I can't seem to leave here anyway." He smiled at me and went out into the little room where people wait to be seated.

I finished my shift and then remembered that Siyo asked me to stop by for lunch. I entered the diner's kitchen with two Styrofoam containers. The extra breakfast food would just go to waste, and the owner doesn't seem to mind me taking some for lunch, so I filled both containers with pancakes, hash browns, and scrambled eggs. I put the containers in a brown bag along with Styrofoam plates and plastic knives and forks. I said my good-byes and met Steve in the waiting area.

Steve sat on the long red vinyl-covered bench where people wait to be seated, next to a hungry-looking senior citizen couple. He stopped browsing through a copy of *NJ Boat Shopper* when he saw me.

"You are from New York. Why are you looking for boats?"

"I live out on Long Island. We have a little bit of water out there, too." He looked up at me with that same adorable smile. "Besides," he continued. "You are fifteen minutes late. But I know, it is not your fault." And he laughed again. His laughter proved contagious and I joined in. I sat down next to him, hoping the smelly greasy outfit I wore would not make him leave right away.

"I had to get lunch for me and my..." I rephrased this into, "I packed up some lunch." Why did I hide that I have a boyfriend? How come I didn't tell him this? I got that same sneaky arousal feeling as being underage in a casino or losing my virginity in an old empty fountain. I don't know if I should feel aroused being sneaky.

"The food smells good," he said. I had hoped the smell of pancakes outweighed the smell of grease coming from my outfit.

"I am taking sailing lessons," Steve continued. "I don't own a sailboat yet, but if I see something for a good price I don't mind picking it up here and taking it with me back to New York. Prices here are expensive though." He stood up and placed the newspaper back on the metal rack.

We talked some more. The waiting room started getting crowded, and I recognized several customers from the after-church crowd. I had to slide closer to him on the bench. My leg pushed against his leg when I swooshed myself over to make room for someone who just came in out of the rain. Electricity! I felt it when my leg touched his. I quickly moved back as much as possible without sitting on the lap of the lady next to me. I blushed.

We talked some more. He asked a lot of questions about me, which I found to be a real turn on. Siyo never asked about me unless one of his sexual incentives were at stake. Steve seemed genuinely interested in knowing more about me. I found Steve very easy to talk with. I learned that he went to Queens College in New York and had lots of friends in New Jersey, hence his frequent trips down this way. I didn't ask if his friends were girls, as that question would cross a line. I did wonder if he had a girlfriend. I knew I should not be thinking like this, but I thought it anyway. I wanted to look somewhere else instead of into his blue eyes, so I turned on my iPhone and realized we'd been talking for over forty minutes.

"Shit!" As soon as it left my mouth, I knew I should have chosen a different response, especially with a few members of the church crowd now staring at me. "I am late to meet my...unless I am mistaken, I think I go right past the entrance to the GSP north. Or maybe it is the Turnpike, I am not too sure. You can follow me. Let's go now, right now. I hate being late." And then, to keep the situation light, I added, "But at least it is your fault I am late and not mine."

"Wait." Steve ripped off a small corner of the boat newspaper he had placed back on the rack. He took out his pen and scribbled on the triangular-shaped paper. "Here's my number. I don't know your situation, but it would be great to see you again. I drive through this way every once in a while, so it would be easy for me to drop by. Maybe we can have lunch together another time."

Tell him you have a boyfriend. Rip up the paper and recycle it. Roll it into a ball and swallow it quickly. Instead though, I nodded and kept the paper, squishing it in the same pocket with all of my tips. That naughty arousal feeling would not leave me. I learned at that moment that a fine line exists between deceit and delight.

We left the restaurant, and he followed me in his old green jaguar. For a few miles, his car stayed right behind mine, but with all of the rain and more cars merging on the road, I no longer saw him in my rearview mirror. The pouring rain made my wipers work overtime making visibility difficult. I thought I did get him to the entrance though, as several miles later I passed an onramp to the GSP northbound.

There were lots of cars, and I found myself going at traffic speeds. People drive so slowly when it rains. I often thought it more dangerous to keep riding your brake in the rain than to just go at a normal speed. *"Sunday drivers,"* I thought to myself. I arrived at Siyo's house over an hour late.

When I knocked on the front door, he opened the door and didn't seem upset at all by my lateness. He gave me a big hug. He didn't even seem to mind the greasy smells of my uniform.

"The pouring rain and lots of Sunday drivers, you know how it is…" I continued blaming the weather and other drivers for my own lateness, when he pressed one of his fingers against my lips for me to shush.

I walked over to the table and saw the same brown bag that he bought in the New Hope costume store. "Why is this here?"

He quickly replied, "Your outfit reeks. Why don't you change into something much cleaner and more comfortable?"

"And revealing?" I added.

"Maybe that, too. I know of a great rainy day activity." He removed a soda can tab from his pocket and smiled an evil sneaky smile. Tab for sex.

I grabbed the tab from his hand and put in my back pocket with the tips. I walked over to the table and opened the brown bag. Surprise, surprise, it contained the costume that he bought in New Hope. I knew by the way he acted in the store that he purchased a costume for me, especially when he hid it from my parents.

The cardboard insert inside the clear plastic wrapper containing this costume had in big black letters *Sexy Nurse Costume,* along with a photo of a girl probably about fourteen years old wearing this outfit.

"How did your mom look in this?" I asked remembering his lie at the costume store register.

"Ha! That response popped out after you put me on the spot like that." He playfully slapped my backside.

"Hmmm, what do you have planned for me?"

"Change into it and find out. We are going to have some fun. I am the patient and you are the nurse. Meet me by that couch."

"What a nice rainy day activity. How about we eat and then play Scrabble instead? Scrabble is a nice rainy day activity, too."

"Jenn, please do your part of the relationship. Remember what we agreed to with those tabs."

"I don't remember giving you another tab." I started to turn red.

"That's not the point. I wait for you all weekend while you work. Can you at least indulge me a little bit? This is a small request."

When does lust turn into love? When does selfishness turn into generosity? I took the costume with me into his bedroom to change.

The costume consisted of a cheap almost see-through version of spandex. He chose an extra-small size for me. I am a small, not an extra small! I knew he did this deliberately.

I stripped down to my panties. This white skimpy cheaply-made nurse costume actually came with a plastic stethoscope. So cheesy!

I put on the costume and tights. It felt so tight on me that I could not even take a deep breath. Not only did it feel uncomfortable, this costume showed everything. I looked at myself in the mirror and let out a small laugh.

The costume fit so tight that my boobs were pushed up, giving me a look even better than the best push-up bra could deliver. The super short skirt exposed the bottom part of my underwear. I'm glad I wore white underwear today. Luckily my white underwear matched and didn't clash with the shade of white in the outfit.

This outfit did make me feel sexy, in a cheap slutty sort of way.

"You are one bizarre boyfriend." I left his bedroom and went back into the living room. When I saw him there I realized he surpassed "bizarre". I found him stretched out on his parents' couch completely naked, looking up at me as I walked over to him.

"Are you okay?" I asked, worried he'd had a heart attack or something. But when I looked down at him, especially his erection, I knew he felt fine, and of course horny.

"You look amazing." Siyo eyed me up and down. "But I am on my last breath. I may need mouth-to-mouth."

"I can help you there," I played along. I put my hand on his forehead, pretending to see if he had a fever. "Yes, very hot. You may need mouth-to-mouth." I leaned over, my hair flopping in his face, causing a little cave where just my lips and his were hiding. I gave him a peck on his lips.

"I-I-I need more," he stammered. "I-I-I think it is helping though."

I kissed him again. This time when I touched his lip, expecting to give him another peck, his mouth opened and he grabbed and squeezed the backs of my legs while he received mouth-to-mouth resuscitation, or more precisely tongue-to-tongue resuscitation.

By the time he released me, I felt like I needed mouth-to-mouth resuscitation for real. I had to catch my breath.

"Feeling better now."

"Good," I replied, catching my breath. "I could never be a real nurse."

"Oh, but you're not done yet. I require more than just mouth-to-mouth. I need your mouth to go somewhere else." When I didn't get what he meant right away, he pointed to his erection.

"Oh," I said. "Mouth-to-dick resuscitation. I'm a professional nurse, mister, not a prostitute. I don't think mouth-to-dick resuscitation is covered by your insurance policy."

"I'm starting to fade again," Siyo's voice trailed off.

"Okay, I can help you. But you will not be able to submit this one through your insurance company. I will consider a barter arrangement." I winked at him and took off my white undies.

"I'll see what I can do," Siyo said, and made several monkey sounds.

I giggled and slowly climbed on top of him positioning my rear in range of his face. I held the bottom of his shaft and licked the top like an ice cream cone. I felt his body tighten. Siyo started squeezing my breasts while licking my backside.

"You get to work now, too. Move that tongue somewhere else," I reminded him. "Pretend you are the monkey."

He continued to squeeze my breasts and started licking me down there. "Faster," I told him.

I got to work, too. Nursing can be tough. I licked up and down his shaft, eventually putting the top of it in my mouth and moving it in and out.

I could feel the pressure building up in my body. "Tell me..." I struggled to finish this sentence as my orgasm neared. "Tell me when you are ready, and I'll get some..." I screamed in delicious agony as I hit my orgasm first. "...paper towels."

"Ready," Siyo stuttered.

"Okay, I think we are all done here," I said. "You seem to be healthy and feeling better. I hope you have the right insurance." I laughed, and he playfully bit my backside.

"Hey! You are going to get an extra charge for that one."

I got two paper towels from the kitchen to keep things neat on his parents' couch. I came back, resumed my position on him, and finished the medical procedure to the sounds of Siyo's familiar "Oh no, oh no, oh no...". I'm glad I grabbed two paper towels. It could have been very messy.

"Sixty-nine is my favorite number," Siyo said afterward, remaining stretched out on the couch naked, watching me put back on my white undies. "I am feeling much better now."

"Pig," I responded. "Another successful day. The nurse saves the patient, and the patient lives to lust after the nurse for another day."

We both got dressed, him in his jeans and T-shirt and me in my greasy and smoky outfit.

When I pulled up my spandex waitress pants, several dollar bills and a ripped piece of paper fell out of my pocket onto the carpet. I picked up the dollar bills but Siyo beat me to the torn piece of paper with Steve's phone number. "Who's Steve?"

"He's a guy I met at the diner, and I helped him with directions." I played down the piece of paper and put the diner food I brought for us on two plates, placed them in the microwave, pressed three minutes and then the Start button. "Are you hungry? I sure am."

He ignored my attempt to change the subject. "Do guys you help with directions always give you their phone numbers?" I could tell he tried to keep an even tone.

"He seemed like a nice guy from New York..." I knew I had said too much. I have a number of friends who are guys and started to explain this to him when Siyo blurted out "If we were both members of my tribe a hundred years ago, and you cheated on me with another warrior, you would be burned at the stake."

"Hey, psycho," I started out, but realized after the words came out of my mouth that I should have taken a much more tactful beginning to such a crucial conversation. "First, this is not a hundred years ago, and second of all, I just got his phone number. We did nothing else." I stayed quiet for a moment and then added, "Look, Siyo, someone came into the diner and asked for directions. We had a nice conversation, and he gave me his phone number. I didn't flip out when you came in to my diner with Amy. You're reading too much into this."

"Am I? But you took his phone number." His voice sounded shaky. "By taking his phone number, you obviously don't think much of our relationship. What would make you take his phone number?"

I couldn't tell Siyo that I kept the piece of paper because I enjoyed that naughty feeling of being sneaky, or maybe I felt something else. Maybe I wanted out of my relationship with Siyo. Maybe Steve learned more about me in forty-five minutes than Siyo did since our first date. I tried to search my brain for psychology studies around self-fulfilling prophecies but came up blank. I didn't know what to say, so I said the first thought on my mind. "Do you love me?"

Siyo had a look of shock on his face. "Why would you ask that question? Do you know how many girls are chasing me and I stuck with you?"

"*Stuck* with me?" I asked, trying to copy his angry tone. "Just answer the question. Do you love me?"

"I can't believe you are turning this all around so it looks like my fault that you cheated on me." Siyo stared me down while saying this.

"You are paranoid, and you don't know what you are about to lose," I said.

"I have phone numbers, too," Siyo said. "I fix houses, and I am around sexy women all of the time. The guys are at work, the women home alone. I have been hit on before."

"We each need some space, at least for a few days," I said, trying to ignore what he just said.

All of a sudden, his demeanor changed and he no longer appeared angry. "You're right," he said. He got up and walked to his bedroom and closed the door behind him. When the door opened, he came over to me and said, "Here." He stretched out his hand to mine and placed about a dozen metal tabs in my palm. "I don't need these anymore. You can give these to Steve to try to get him to sleep with you."

"Flattery will get you nowhere." I took the metal tabs. How much soda does he drink? Siyo clenched his other hand in a fist. "You best be leaving." He stood up and stretched both arms out, requesting a hug. His right hand remained in a fist. As I walked into his embrace, he unclenched his right hand and before I could back off, he grabbed my hand and pricked my palm with a sharp point of the dream snatcher he had hid. I recoiled in pain. Blood started dripping from my palm.

I stared at him with a look of surprise.

"If you thought your dreams were kinky and strange before, wait till tonight's dream." He laughed a short angry laugh. "Time for you to go, Jenn. See you in your dreams."

My emotions had toggled from being angry at myself, to being angry at Siyo, to blaming fate, to feeling sorry for Siyo, and now back to being angry at Siyo. "I just gave you a blow job and this is the thanks I get?"

"Take the blame. You did this, Jenn, not me. You will be losing the best thing you had – me. You will be crawling back to me, I know."

"You perverted pompous psycho! I wish we never met to begin with!" Tears formed, and I wiped them off quickly. I took the piece of paper with Steve's phone number off the table and left without looking back.

During the short drive home, I started feeling more and more anger toward Siyo. I picked up my cell phone and called the number on the ripped piece of paper. "Hi," Steve answered.

"Hi, this is Jenn." I said my name because I realized he did not have my phone number in his address book, so he would not know who called.

"Jenn, did you know you led me to the Turnpike instead of the GSP? This is the second time you screwed up with directions. I thought the first time you gave me bad directions on purpose just to get me back to the diner. Are you calling to apologize for this second mistake or to blame me in some way?"

He stayed quiet for a moment. Today just kept getting worse and worse. I couldn't have Steve angry at me, too. I tried to think of something to say to fix the situation.

"Got you! I am just kidding, Jenn, I followed you and found the GSP North entrance, just like you said. Just joking with you." I heard his little boy laugh.

"Funny," I replied. *Not exceptionally funny.*

"I think so."

"So what are you doing Sunday?" I asked him. So much for me playing hard to get. I felt anger toward Siyo and at the same time I wanted to see Steve. Maybe I should be with Steve.

"Are you asking me out for a date? If yes, I know a good diner. A cute waitress with a poor sense of direction works there." He laughed again.

"No diners. I will call you later in the week to firm up plans."

"I like a woman who takes charge," he said.

After the call, I couldn't help but smile. I didn't know if I felt happy because Steve seemed to make me smile, or because I somehow wanted to get even with Siyo. Either way, I smiled all the way home.

When I got back home, I recycled all of those metal tabs – they were recyclables after all! I turned on the shower faucets in preparation for a steamy shower.

I wanted to explain this situation to somebody. I couldn't talk to my parents for sure. I tried to imagine how the conversation would go with my parents. *Mom and Dad, let me just get this out on the table. Siyo has fucked me several times. He also has been acting out some of his dark fantasies on me in my dreams. What's your advice?* Not going to happen.

I finished my shower and got dressed into pajamas. I put some hydrogen peroxide on my new cut and covered it with a Band-Aid.

I had a quiet dinner with my parents and then went to bed, trying to comfort myself that whatever Siyo had planned, it would just be a dream.

I am walking through the aisles of a busy marketplace. This marketplace is definitely not in New Jersey, maybe somewhere in the Middle East or India. Men around me are wearing robes and sandals, and most have turbans. There is a murmur of a language I have never heard before as the sellers and buyers conduct their business.

I look at the tables and stands as I walk by and see lots of strange items being sold, most of these items probably illegal in the United States. To my right, I notice a man paying a vendor and reaching for a small monkey in a cage. The monkey is shrieking. I hope that monkey will become that man's pet and not his dinner.

To my left as I continue to walk, a heated negotiation is taking place between a buyer and seller over the price of a caged miniature white horse, about a foot tall.

I notice many strange foods, too, such as a vegetable that is carrot-shaped but dark blue in color, and something that could be blueberries if they were not neon yellow. Definitely not the typical Jersey flea market.

The sandy ground feels hot against my feet, and the bright sun makes me squint. Maybe I can find sandals and a hat, or maybe suntan lotion, although that is unlikely, as they just sell out-of-the-ordinary freaky finds.

As I continue to walk up and down the aisles, becoming more and more amazed by what is for sale, I also become aware that I am not wearing much – just a neon red string bikini. I am not even wearing a ponytail holder, which makes my long hair cover part of my bare back.

I wish I had long enough hair to cover my entire body, like Cousin It from the Addams Family. I wouldn't feel so exposed.

My outfit is in sharp contrast to everyone else's. The men have robes covering almost all of their skin, I am wearing the same bikini I tried on in New Hope that Siyo picked out for me, the one I modeled to embarrass him in front of my parents. Although I am surrounded by hundreds of strange men, nobody appears to be looking at me. They all seem to be involved in their own affairs.

I approach the end of one of the aisles and instead of a table that contains lots of wares or food for sale, a vendor is sitting cross-legged on a pillow in the center of a large red and black checkered rug next to a light brown woven basket.

He motions for me to come closer and smiles when I take a step forward. He is old with a long gray beard and his smile reveals many missing teeth. He should smile with his mouth closed. He is wearing a faded blue turban and white robe.

I take a few more steps forward out of curiosity, so that my feet are half on the rug and half on the sandy ground. I try to say, "What's in the basket?" but no sounds come out. He seems to understand though. He picks up a wooden flute, puts it to his mouth and starts to play.

The music sounds like the instrumental music from an *Indiana Jones* movie. It is pleasant, and I turn around, surprised to see I am the only one listening to him play. I would rather hear this free song then try to negotiate for a shrieking monkey.

The basket cover starts shifting. Then the cover slowly starts rising. I take a small step back, so my feet are completely on the sandy ground. I notice a triangular-shaped yellow snake head emerge from the basket. Its tongue is lengthening and retracting, the bright red eyes of the snake are fixated on me.

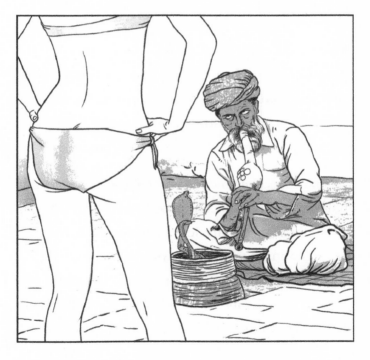

The snake's head looks silly under the straw cover, as if the snake is wearing the cover as a hat. The head moves slowly from side to side as it comes out of the basket. The head belongs to a large snake with yellow and black bands. The straw cover falls onto the rug as the snake keeps rising, eventually plopping out of the basket and onto the rug.

I turn from side to side and notice I am still the only person watching. What a great show people are missing! I have never seen a snake move to music. As the old flutist continues to play, the snake starts moving – this time toward me!

"Mister, get your snake back in the basket!" He does not seem to hear me. I realize I am done with this show, and take one or two steps backward, but the snake is coming toward me quicker than I can retreat. I try to scream but no sound comes out.

The snake reaches me and wraps itself around my ankles. The old man continues to play as the snake starts climbing up my legs. The old man nods at me, signaling that he knows what the snake is doing and ignoring my pleas. It travels around my legs as it works its way higher to my calves and then to my thighs. It is a long, thick snake, and I feel its weight on my body as it works its way up to my waist. I try to push it down and off me, hoping the snake will not bite me. The thick scaly rubbery snake will not budge.

The snake passes a second time around my waist and tightens its grip, like a belt in its smallest setting. I motion to the flutist, "Look what your snake is doing!" but he continues to play.

The head of the snake rises up to my face. His triangular face seems to be grinning. His narrow long tongue goes in and out of his mouth, almost to the beat of the music. He tightens his grip around my waist even more. As he tightens his grip, he grins even more. I try to say, "Hey, what are you doing?" but nothing comes out. Why can't I talk?

The snake then lowers its gaze, now eyeing my chest. As I try to loosen the scaly belt from my waist, I feel the snake's thin tongue lick the bottom of my breasts. The string bikini top does a lousy job of covering my breasts, but that's the idea, isn't it? My breasts are fully exposed, top and bottom, just my nipples are covered with the string. The snake licks across the bottom part of my breasts and then the top part, slowly dragging his tongue against my skin in a circular pattern. It feels like wet sandpaper being scraped across my breasts.

The old man changes the tempo slightly on his flute and the snake starts moving its sandpapery tongue from my breasts down to my belly, licking to the beat of the music. I feel the wet sandpaper pass over my belly button and continue south. The string bikini does an even worse job of covering that area, and I feel this firsthand as the wet sandpaper glides over my sex and works its way between my legs.

A large part of the snake passes between my legs, rubbing right in that very sensitive spot as it slowly slithers to my backside. I gasp, or at least try to gasp — nothing comes out. The snake is widest in its middle, and I am forced to spread my legs to let the thicker parts of the snake pass through.

The old man's tempo changes once again. The snake traces a thin wet circular pattern on my bottom. A feature of a string bikini is that everything is nicely visible, especially to horny snakes with sandpapery tongues.

The old man than plays a single loud note and the snake obeys, causing an intensely sharp pain, like someone applying a staple remover on my ass.

Shit! I look over my shoulder and realize I have experienced my first snake bite. The snake continues to bite down as it grins up at me, like an old toothless man with a mouth full of food.

I feel faint from the snake's venom. I can longer move my arms or legs. I am completely frozen! That snake's venom has paralyzed me!

I still can feel, but I cannot move. The music stops. I feel the snake's fangs release, and then, just as quick as the snake climbed up me, the snake loosens its hold and slithers back to its home in the basket.

I am frozen now, staring at the old man with the flute at his side. I see that toothless smile again. He stands up, then bends over and picks up the basket cover. He fastens it tightly to the top of the basket, the snake safely inside. He moves the small pillow he had sat on closer to the front of the rug.

Then he starts walking toward me, his smile even wider than before. He must have only five teeth in his entire mouth.

He stops in front of me.

He stretches his wrinkly pointy hands out toward me and squeezes my breasts. He does this while maintaining eye contact with me, and with his eyes tells me, "Look what I can do to you. You can't stop me. How many strange men have ever squeezed your big tits before? I must be the first. You are mine, I can touch you and do whatever I want to you."

He then walks around me, letting his long and probably filthy nails lightly scrape against my skin. I feel his hands on my hair and then he slowly works his way down my back to my backside. His hands rest there for a moment, and then he gives my backside a full two-handed shameless squeeze.

After getting his jollies, he puts one hand between my legs and one hand across my breasts and lifts me effortlessly, like how a horny department store employee would lift a manikin. He carries me back to his rug and places me face down, so that the small pillow is under the front of my bikini, and my bottom is elevated.

I feel a sharp slap on my butt. Did the old guy just spank me? I think so. He spanks me a few more times, and I feel the sting from the hot redness on my cheeks. If I could only move, I could defend myself and knock out his remaining teeth.

He then calls out to the marketplace something in his foreign tongue. I do not understand what he is saying, but he is loud and I can guess it has to do with me and my elevated ass.

A crowd is forming around me. I cannot move my head so I can only tell this by staring at the many pairs of mens' sandals. My "owner" continues to shout to the crowd, and I can tell the crowd is staring at my backside, probably now a light shade of red where I had been slapped.

I hear a voice, a familiar voice, but in a foreign language and the men part. I know they give way because I see the sandals step back and a single pair of sandals move in. I can hear the two men talking, and then it occurs to me that the other voice I am hearing is Siyo! My knight in shining armor. I will be saved!

It seems some money is being exchanged. I see Siyo's sandals move toward my face and Siyo comes down to my level and looks at me. "Poor Jenn," he says. "All frozen and no place to go. Should I rescue you? Or should I punish you and give you what you deserve for breaking up our relationship."

He has not come to rescue me, after all.

I try to say "Fuck you," but nothing comes out.

Then he sits down near my backside and with all of the men watching me, he slaps me! And hard! In the same place the old guy slapped me! He spanks me again, and again, and again. "Fifty spanks for leaving your boyfriend," I hear him say.

The crowd counts in their foreign tongue, or at least I am guessing that's what they are doing since I don't know one fucking word they are saying. All I know is that there is a sharp sting every time his hand hits my bottom, and he seems to be slapping harder and harder. He is slapping in the same area, again and again. If I am going to get spanked, at least do it in different spots, spread the pain. Please!

I consider myself a tough person, but after he hits number twenty, tears start to roll down my face. Thirty is agonizing. The only pain that hurts more than the physical pain of the slaps is the humiliation. It feels awful to be spanked in front of what must be at least a hundred men.

I have never been spanked before. Not even when my parents were so angry after I confessed to starting a small fire with a magnifying glass in Jimmy's backyard when we were eight.

I try to think of other thoughts, such as the fire I started at Jimmy's, and this makes me get to forty. By the time fifty arrives, I am screaming to myself with every slap. I am physically in a lot of pain but I also feel disgraced.

He turns me over so we are making eye contact. The pressure of my bruised backside against the rug increases my pain. Siyo grins. "I am not done with you yet, Jenn."

He flips me back over.

"Who wants to see her tits?" he asks the crowd. As the men gather closer, he unfastens my bikini top.

He turns me once again on my back and displays my breasts to the appreciative crowd.

I can't take this any longer. I focus my energy, and I can feel my fingers moving. With all my strength, I knee Siyo as hard as I can right between his legs. He groans and clenches his crotch in pain. He gives me a look of surprise and shock.

I wake up with a feeling of power and also freedom.

Arugula Avocado – Awesome!

I am a salad person. Arugula is one of the oldest aphrodisiacs in the book, going back to the first century! The minerals and antioxidants found in dark leafy greens like arugula have been proven to strengthen libido. Add chunks of fresh avocado to your salad and you have the sure thing. Avocado contains Vitamin E which will increase your endurance during sex.

Now for the icing on the cake, sprinkle some pine nuts on top. They are incredibly high in zinc, which have been linked to a healthy sex drive. For over the top sex, add basil to your salad, too. Don't you just love the smell of basil? The great smell of basil can actually have an aphrodisiac effect on you and your partner.

Second Chance?

I have social studies and Spanish on Mondays, and with my seat right next to Siyo's, I knew today would be awkward. I did not look at him or speak with him in either class. He approached me after Spanish.

"Jenn, about last night."

"That dream proved once again you think with your dick and not with your heart. If you care about me just even a little you would have introduced romance, if not in real life than at least in my dream. Like a romantic vacation on a Caribbean Island. Did you actually get off on having a snake bite me and then a toothless old man spank me?" There I said it, and hopefully I said it quiet enough for no one else to hear.

"I did," Siyo whispered. "And look, I'm sorry. I sometimes get carried away. I felt angry at you for taking some guy's phone number. I'll tell you what. I know I don't deserve any more chances, but if you give me one more chance, the Caribbean islands it will be. I will make sure it is romantic. I will try hard to think with my heart."

My brain screamed *run*, yet my heart countered with *he wants to try*.

"One more chance, please."

My heart won over my brain. I stretched my hand out to him to be cut once again. "Love, not lust," I said, more to try to convince me than to change him.

The sun is beating down on Siyo and me as we walk toward the hotel pool with snorkel gear and beach towels in hand. Our hotel is a grand beach resort, right out of a travel magazine, everything is luxurious and spacious.

Just beyond the pool is the Caribbean Sea with its crystal blue waters. After practicing snorkeling in the pool, I will explore the sea life.

The cement walkway feels hot against my bare feet. I am wearing a bright pink bikini and Siyo is wearing black swimming trunks. We drop our towels on lounge chairs and put on our flippers. We laugh as we walk in our flippers, like two penguins waddling to the pool's edge.

We sit on the edge of the pool and put our legs in. The water feels warm, cooler than the air but still warm.

Siyo pushes himself in off the side of the pool and goes right under. He comes up and grabs me by the waist, and as I say "No, I need a few more minutes," he grins and drags me into the pool and dunks me under the water, his hands still on my waist.

"Hey, not fair," I say when he pulls me up. He gives me a light kiss on the lips. I don't see anyone else around the pool, so my self-conscious takes a back seat and I return a big kiss.

After several more big kisses, Siyo says, "Let's practice diving down to the bottom of the deep end of this pool." He fastens his mask and inserts his snorkel and does a perfect dive to the bottom. He shows off his form as his tan muscular body heads toward the depths of the pool.

He touches the bottom and a moment later goes close to the surface and blows the water out of his snorkel, still staying under the water while he breathes through the snorkel.

I know it takes practice to continue staying under the water after a dive, but I also know that by his hand signal pointing down, he is telling me that it is my turn. I put on my mask and place the snorkel in my mouth, and then dive under the water.

I feel a gentle pat on my backside, as a sign of encouragement from Siyo, or maybe he intended it to be a push down to the bottom of the pool. Either way, I make it to the bottom. I could tell he is watching me the whole way down, my body thrusting toward the bottom, my legs spreading wide apart as I propel myself deeper and deeper.

I come up and repeat what Siyo had done. I blow through the snorkel and stay under the water. It is easier than I imagined. We are both staring at each other and then he mumbles through his snorkel, "Let's see who can stay under the longest." I like a challenge.

We keep staring at each other under the water while breathing through our snorkels, and it is definitely a stand still. I then reach out and try to make him laugh by tickling him as an attempt to win this game. He laughs a little but not enough to get him to come up to the surface.

Siyo then reaches his arms out and pulls down my bikini top, just enough so it pushes up my breasts, like a red-eyed sea monster with big bulgy eyes, staring at him. I start laughing through my snorkel, a self-conscious laughter, and I can tell my face is bright red. Before I can pull my top back up, he cups his hands over my breasts and gives a squeeze, and tickles my nipples with his thumbs.

"You win, you win," I try to signal with my hands, but he shows no sign of stopping.

I finally come to the surface and take my snorkel out. We are in the deep end so I am treading water. "Enough already, I give up."

Siyo finally stops his antics and comes to the surface too. He pulls me closer and kisses me, and my hands are locked at my sides so I cannot even pull up my top. I feel his muscular chest against my exposed bosom, and his hands clamp to my bottom so I don't have to tread water.

This would have been even more romantic if we were not still wearing our masks, as our lips are touching but there is a constant colliding of plastic. We find ourselves laughing and trying to kiss at the same time.

After several minutes of this light-hearted foreplay, he lets go of my arms so I can raise my bikini top and we get out of the pool, take our masks and flippers off, and stretch out on the lounge chairs.

It felt wonderful to dry on our chairs in the sun.

"Isn't this great?" Siyo asks.

"Loving it," I reply.

"You do know I want to have sex with you now?" Siyo says, stretching out on his lounge chair, displaying a blatant erection. "But," he continues, "our relationship is much more than physical, so let's just relax on these lounge chairs."

I say nothing, just stretch out on my lounge chair.

"I would like to rub my hands all of the way from your hair down to your toes. I would enjoy sucking on your nipples and feeling the warm moist feeling of being deep inside of you. I like the thought of violating you, doing things to you that your parents would not approve of in a million years."

He catches himself and wipes off small flecks of white foam that have formed around the corner of his mouth. "But, I won't. Yes, there is more to our relationship than sex. Jenn, why don't you snorkel a bit in the sea? It will give me a chance to recharge and focus on other thoughts, and you a chance to practice your snorkeling."

"You want me to leave you? I am not ruling sex out. I do feel exposed here but maybe we could go back to the hotel room."

"No sex," Siyo says firmly. "I need to see if I can…if we have something worth more than sex. Besides you might see some fish that you will not see anywhere else in the world."

While walking to the water, I run my finger inside the back of my bikini bottom and adjust it ever so slightly. When I remove my finger, I hear the sound of spandex against skin, and I turn back to see Siyo ogling me, wanting me. I did not have to turn around to know that he had been staring at me. Why he did not want to have sex is beyond me.

The warm sand feels great on my feet and in between my toes. As I reach the wetter sand near the ocean, small waves lap up to my ankles, and then recede. The water feels cool, but not cold. It is the same temperature as the pool.

I keep walking in, the water now up to my waist. No matter how warm the water is, it always feels cold when it reaches my belly button. I shiver and feel my nipples harden through my bikini top.

I snap the goggles around my face, put my mouth over the snorkel, and dip my head in the water. I float and kick my flippers, looking down into the sea. It is so beautiful to see the world under the waves, like I'm peering into some other planet. It is quiet, just the sound of my own breathing through the tube. The rocks and greenery at the bottom make it seem like I am hovering over a completely different world.

I see a school of bright yellow fish. As they swim by me, they all turn blue, and then moments later red and back to yellow again. The hundreds of fish change to the same color at the same time. Where is my camera when I need it? Unbelievable.

Small pieces of seaweed flutter past me, like green butterflies. I know seaweed is not alive, but these pieces seem to be swarming around me, gently brushing by my body as I snorkel above them. I can barely see the sandy sea bottom through all of this greenery.

I decide to keep snorkeling in the same direction, hoping this thick layer of seaweed will eventually be behind me. I lose sight of the bottom and am not even sure whether I am going further out to sea or toward the shore. This thought scares me, and I start breathing rapidly through the snorkel. I can be far from shore, maybe in twenty or thirty feet deep of water. It could take a while to get back. But before I get too worried, I emerge from the swarm of seaweed butterflies and again see the bottom.

I sigh through the snorkel realizing I am not far from the shore after seeing the bottom, which looks shallow enough for me to stand. A large hermit crab with a neon purple shell scurries by on the sandy bottom. Once again, I relax and enjoy the view.

The water continues to get shallower, so I must be getting closer to shore. When I am in about waist-deep water, I spot the tip of what looks like a tentacle on the sandy bottom. It is greenish-brown and I wonder if it is going to change colors like those fish.

I continue to snorkel, tracing the tentacle to its source. and must belong to a big octopus, as the tentacle is getting thicker and is even wider than my thigh. I notice other tentacles, too. I count more than ten tentacles but it could be less because the tentacles are piled on top of each other, like massive slugs tied together in an orgy.

I keep snorkeling, kicking my feet and then realize that maybe it is not so wise to keep going ahead. Are octopuses safe to get this close to? Can't they shoot some murky liquid at their prey? Is this even an octopus?

However, I am more curious than frightened, so I keep moving ahead, kicking my flippers with my arms at my side.

Now the water is shallow enough where the tips of my flippers are touching the tentacles when I kick each one down. The tentacles do not move as the rubber flippers make contact. Maybe these tentacles are part of the fossil remains of a creature long dead.

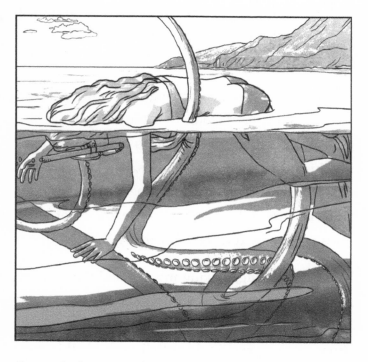

One of the tentacles resting on top of another tentacle is so close to me as I snorkel above it that my bikini top brushes hard against it. My breasts press against the rough tentacle. Of the two, my breasts or the tentacle, it is my breasts that accommodate and get compressed against the rough tentacle.

Then this tentacle moves ever so slightly. Just enough so that the suction part of the tentacle fits between my skin and my bikini top and the bikini top snaps off my body. The tentacle pulls my bikini top out of my reach and then out of my site.

I am topless! In a state of shock, I stand up to locate my bikini top so I can put it back on quickly. When I stand up, I became aware of two facts: my feet are balancing on those rough tentacles, and I am flashing everyone on the shore.

I quickly jump back under the water, my snorkel still in my mouth. I am more self-conscious than I am scared. Although I did not see my bikini top, I scoped out where Siyo is sitting by the pool. If I could snorkel in that direction, I could yell from the water for Siyo to bring me a towel so I can cover myself without drawing much attention.

When I return under the water, I also remind myself that the tentacle moved, meaning these tentacles I am snorkeling on top of belong to something big that is also alive.

I put this thought out of my mind as I start kicking in a different direction toward the shore. My fins continue to make contact with those tentacles, this time sharply as I kick hard to move fast toward shore. Maybe I'll spot my bikini top as I make my way to the beach.

I feel a tentacle tip between my flippers and ankles and moments later both flippers slide off my feet.

My flippers are floating somewhere, too. I am topless and flipperless. I can't stand up to locate my flippers and top, or everyone on the shore gets a booby show again. I am closer to the shore than before, so those watching will get an even better show. I instead start snorkeling around, hoping I will see my bikini top or flippers on the surface and grab them and put them back on.

I turn around and sure enough, my flippers are about twenty feet ahead of me, floating on the surface, a little past where I had snorkeled before. I quickly start kicking my feet, and this time also using my hands to push me, as I move a lot slower without flippers. My feet touch the tentacles, and they feel like frozen slimy rubber.

Both flippers are floating just a little further in front of me. I stretch out my arms to reach for them at the same time I glance down into the water. I see what all of those tentacles are attached to – a large oval head with eyes looking up at me!

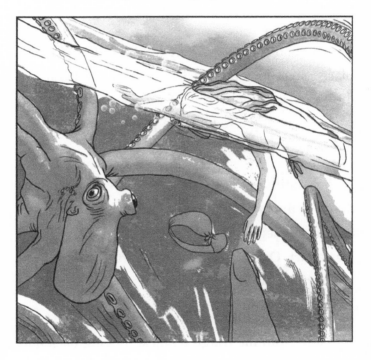

His bulging eyes are far apart and slightly off-centered from each other. A wide slit underneath his eyes must be his mouth. The giant octopus' face is heavily wrinkled and covered with barnacles.

His head is huge, about the size of those exercise balls I do sit-ups on at the gym.

I stretch my arms out to grab my flippers, which are floating on the surface just out of reach ahead of me. As I do, this creature stretches its head up just slightly as it is in range of my body, and the slit that I correctly guessed to be his mouth opens and fastens firmly over an entire boob.

Two of its tentacles grab my thighs and hold me in place as the octopus sucks aggressively from my nipple. It is actually less of a suck and more like someone taking a toilet bowl plunger and pushing it repeatedly against my breast.

As he continues to pump or suck or whatever he is doing to my breast, his other tentacles start to wrap around my legs and waist. He effortlessly pulls my legs apart. One of his tentacles starts rubbing back and forth between my legs.

Even though I still have my bikini bottom on, I feel pressure from the rough tentacle moving back and forth against my sex. My body becomes tighter and tighter. I am breathing fast short breaths through the small tube. The combination of sensations on my breast and sex, along with the feeling of those suction-cupped tentacles wrapped tightly around my body, make me give an orgasmic scream through my mouthpiece. The sounds of muffled "ooooohs!" and "yeses!" through a fourteen-inch plastic tube must sound like a whale mating call to anyone who might have heard nearby. I just hope no whales misinterpret my sounds. This is my first orgasmic snorkeling adventure.

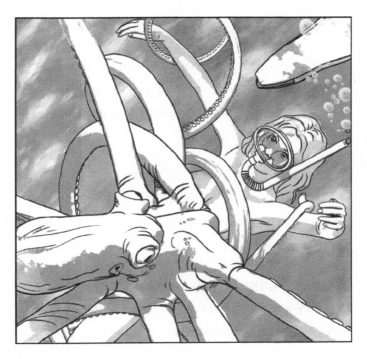

I fatigue and put my hands by my side, actually alongside his tentacles by my side. Do whatever you want to me and hopefully more like you just did.

After several minutes of plunging one breast, his mouth releases and then without hesitating moves on to my yet untouched breast. His slit-like mouth opens and sucks in my other breast, like sucking in a large bubble gum bubble.

His grip remains steadfast on my body, and again I feel that sensation between my legs as he pleasures me. My body reacts to him, getting tight before exploding into another orgasm.

I am completely spent. He removes his mouth from my breast. Then he begins to loosen his grip around my body. One by one, the tentacles release me.

He is not holding me at all now. I am exhausted and have to get back to the shore. In front of me are my flippers and I am able to grab them and quickly put them on my feet.

I kick my flippers, careful not to scrape against the tentacles too much. I seem to be a bit lighter in the water, and looking down at my chest I see why. I am completely flat-chested! That creature had sucked everything from my breasts. I gasp underwater. Then I stand up and see my bikini top in the near distance. I reach for it quickly and put it back on. It is a lot looser than normal, and I take off my flippers when I reach ankle deep water. I start walking rapidly back to Siyo while he watches me approach, still sitting in that same chaise lounge chair.

I walk up to him, upset that my shapely breasts are no more.

"Did you enjoy the snorkeling?" Siyo asks not acknowledging my loose-fitting bikini top.

"If you didn't notice, I wasn't flat chested when I went in to snorkel." I am holding up the bikini top with my hands, realizing it is so loose it will probably just fall off.

"Jenn, I didn't even know until you just brought it up. I love you for you, not for your body. I don't care about breast size. That is just so skin-deep. I care about you, not what you look like. How shallow a person do you think I am? Here, lay next to me a little bit. I just want to be with you."

I am speechless. He is so sweet. I lean back on his lounge chair and with his arms around me, I close my eyes and fall asleep.

I awoke and am alone in my bedroom.

Now that's the type of dream I like. Siyo is learning, I hope, but it may be too late.

Orgasmic Asparagus

Asparagus might not seem like such an amorous vegetable, but history tells a different tale. Nicholas Culpepper, an English herbalist from the 1600s, wrote that asparagus "stirs up lust in man and woman." In 19th century France, brides and grooms were served three courses of asparagus during their wedding dinner to improve performance during their first night as husband and wife. Asparagus contains lots of sensual goodies including folic acid, which makes it easier for both men and woman to reach orgasm.

Preheat the oven to 450 degrees. Combine two tablespoons each of garlic oil, balsamic vinegar, mustard, and honey, with one pound of asparagus and roast until crisp (about fifteen minutes).

This is a two-punch recipe because you not only get the romantic benefits of asparagus, but also honey which helps regulate estrogen and testosterone levels and provides a natural energy boost.

End of the Rainbow

Tuesday went a lot smoother than Monday in both social studies and Spanish. Siyo and I chatted excitedly before and after class.

"Did you like the dream last night?" Siyo asked while we were walking home together.

"I did. I like that the dream's theme did not revolve around sex or some dark fetish of yours. Although, that octopus bordered on the cusp of being naughty. Actually it was very, very, naughty, but part of me definitely got off on it. A small part. Maybe you are becoming a romantic. I especially like that you didn't just want to jump my bones."

"Okay. I am starting to understand. I need to practice more."

"What do you mean?" I asked.

"Let me give you another dream tonight. Maybe if I can learn through my dreams, I can learn through real life. I can become even more romantic. Does that make sense?"

"I guess. I don't want any weird creatures though. Just you and me. Okay?"

"I'll try," Siyo said and when we reached his house, we went inside so he could get the snatcher and a Band-Aid. He reopened an existing cut, and I squirmed only slightly.

Siyo gave me a kiss goodbye on my forehead, and when I left his house my phone rang. I let it ring. When I got to the end of Siyo's walkway, I took out my phone and saw I missed a call from Steve. I called him right back.

"Can't wait to see you Sunday," Steve said.

"What would you like to do?" I asked as I walked at a brisk pace toward home, trying not to think of Siyo.

"How about we hang out in Seaside and then do Mexican food? I am skilled at some of the boardwalk games and I know I can win you some prizes."

"Sounds like fun," I said and gave him my address. "Pick me up around three. I am pretty good at some of those games too, so maybe you'll go home with a stuffed animal as well!"

I felt funny about going on a date with Steve when it wasn't fully over with Siyo. Siyo has made effort to think more with his heart. On the other hand, I did not want to miss an opportunity to get to know Steve better, especially because he seemed to truly want to get to know me and not just my body.

My mom and I brought dinner to my dad at the pharmacy and then afterward I decided to call it an early night, excited to see what Siyo had planned for me. I did not fear tonight's dream.

I am riding a white horse. Siyo is riding a brown horse alongside me. We are galloping, racing each other and laughing. My hair is blowing wildly in the wind.

We follow a narrow trail. As I speed by Siyo, he smiles at me and I admire his muscular build as he is only wearing shorts. He is behind me now, and I feel him eyeing me in my jeans and bikini top as I bounce up and down in the saddle.

We stop when we reach a clearing. There is a crystal clear lake being fed from a waterfall. We get off our horses and tie them to a nearby tree.

I walk over to admire the waterfall and lake. It is right out of a *Fantasy Island* episode. The sounds of falling water on rocks, and birds chirping fill the air. I take a deep break and inhale the delicious surroundings.

I feel Siyo's arm around my waist, and he pulls me back toward him. I feel his erection against my backside and turn around and see that in the time I admired the lake, he has pulled off his shorts and set up a picnic blanket.

There doesn't appear to be anyone else around, so I take off my jeans and panties. "What do you have in mind?" I ask him.

He leads me toward the blanket. "Lay down," he says.

I lay on my back and he gets down on his knees between my legs. I pivot my waist up toward him, arching my back and balancing on my shoulders and neck.

He enters me and closes his eyes in ecstasy.

"What are you going to do now, little piggy?" I ask.

"Just enjoying this feeling for moment." His eyes are still closed.

I start slowly moving my thighs up and down, and Siyo starts moving in and out.

He is touching a certain spot deep inside of me when he pushes all of the way forward. I push up, and it feels amazing.

Before it becomes anything more though, I hear the familiar pleading from Siyo. "Oh no, oh no, oh no…" He releases inside of me.

After a few moments, he lays down alongside me.

"I'm glad one of us is satisfied." My sarcastic tone is evident.

He stands up and pulls me up. "Let's cool off a bit," he says and picks me up in his arms and walks into the lake while holding me tightly in the cradle position. We are still both nude, with the exception of my bikini top.

Siyo walks into the water until he reaches about waist deep. Without a word, he drops me into the icy cold water. I go right under and it is hard to breathe it is so cold. I come up shivering, and I hear him laughing.

"Not funny," I say and jab him in his tight abs.

"Ah, I will make it up to you. I'm going to teach you the alphabet." He takes a deep breath and holds it, and then goes under the water.

I feel his tongue circle my belly button once before continuing its journey further south. When I feel his tongue licking the hairs between my legs, I close my eyes.

Siyo starts licking to the pattern of each letter of the alphabet. I feel the letter 'A' being engraved down there, while Siyo's hands tightly grip my butt. Now 'B'. The letters continue. I love the letter 'E' for its complexity and of course 'G'. 'I' is my least favorite. My eyes remain closed as I feel each licked letter further tighten my body. I wonder if I can make it to 'Z'. 'J' has me on the edge, and I start to scream as 'K' sends me into a climax.

Siyo removes his tongue and hands and comes up for air. I realize that he held his breath under the water for quite some time.

"Now we're even." He grins, hugging me tightly, two naked bodies in the cool lake.

We walk out of the water, hand in hand.

I lay down on my belly, the sun feeling good on my back and warming me.

"As tired as I am, I will not waste this moment," Siyo says, standing above me, separating my legs slightly on the blanket.

"Haven't you had enough, piggy?"

"I thought I did. But you shouldn't lie down on your stomach, teasing me like this." He playfully slaps my backside.

"It's not all about you," I tell him.

"But it is," he responds. "You should be flattered whenever I want your body. If you deny me, someone else will quickly fill your place. Did you know Amy asked to come with me today? But I chose you. Please don't throw away this opportunity."

I consider this. "Fine, but make it quick, piggy," I say, knowing it will be quick anyway.

I feel Siyo spread my legs further and then feel him inside of me once again. His movements are slower than before, yet with each thrust he pushes as deep as he can.

He starts increasing his speed and sure enough, again the pleading, and shortly after his water gun goes off inside of me.

"Don't make me do that again," Siyo says grinning, and slaps my backside playfully once again. He turns over and closes his eyes.

"Don't worry, I'll make sure to lie down on my back next time." I give his stomach a playful slap.

"Hey," he says, "I'm trying to rest."

"I am going to wash off." I get up and go back into the cold water and come out clean.

I walk back to Siyo, who is asleep and breathing deeply. I look at his naked body stretched out. He has no shame. I am no longer tired after plunging back into the cold water. After drying off, I get dressed back into my jeans and bikini top.

In the distance, I see a beautiful rainbow. Bright clear colors. Usually rainbows fade at some point along their curve, but this rainbow has the same vivid colors all the way through.

The rainbow seems to end in the not so far distance. A voice in my head tells me to try to find the pot of gold at the end of that rainbow. This is the kind of place where you would expect to find a pot of gold, so tropical and magical.

Siyo is fast asleep, so I can be the explorer and see what is at the end of the rainbow and still be back before he wakes up. I don't think he will miss me anyway. He got what he wanted – twice!

I untie and mount my horse, and start riding toward the end of the rainbow. It is a perfect day for a horseback ride. As I ride through the thick forest, light shines through the gaps between the leaves on the high branches.

I bounce up and down on the saddle, my hair waving in the air as my horse trots through the narrow path in the woods. I keep following the path, hoping it will eventually open up into a clearing where I can track that rainbow again. I hope it is nearby.

I notice as the ride continues that the forest is getting darker. The taller trees allow only shards of light to enter, adding eeriness to the surroundings. I wonder if I should have gone on this adventure.

But at that moment, I notice the rainbow through the trees and it appears that I am not that far away after all. I continue along the trail and remind myself of the saying, "It's always darkest just before dawn." In this case it's true, as right up ahead I see the trail full of light. When I emerge from the thick canopy, I am in a large clearing.

I survey the beautiful surroundings. In the center of the clearing, the rainbow touches the meadow. It is just like a fairy tale, bright blues, yellows, reds, and purples all touching the emerald green grass.

I notice something at the point where the rainbow touches the ground. I tie up my horse and walk over to what looks like a large black bowling ball. When I walk close enough, I see that it is a black cauldron filled to the rim with shiny gold coins!

I blink several times, wondering if I am seeing things, but each time I open my eyes the pot filled with coins is still there. The fairy tales are true – there is a pot of gold at the end of the rainbow!

A spooky feeling comes over me and I shiver. It is completely quiet, not even the sounds of birds or the wind to break the silence. I decide to quickly take my treasure and scram. I bend over to pick up the pot, but as soon as I lift it off the ground, the rainbow disappears and I feel an extremely sharp pain on my backside.

I spin around, carefully clutching the heavy treasure to my chest and don't see anything.

Then I look directly down and smiling up at me is what could only be a leprechaun. He is rubbing his stubby thumb and pointer, the two fingers which I am certain were guilty of painfully pinching my behind.

"Asshole," I shout down at him and rub my backside, hoping the hurt will subside.

The little man, probably no more than three feet tall, looks old, even ancient, but he has large green bright eyes that look timeless. His smile did not fade after I cursed at him. It is as if he didn't hear me at all. He holds a pipe in his mouth with the hand that did not inflict pain to my bottom.

He has a bright red beard, like strawberry cotton candy pasted all over his face. He wears a large three-pointed hat that covers up to his bushy bright red eyebrows.

He says in a melodic tone, "Aren't ends beautiful? The rainbow's end. Your rear end." His Irish accent is charming. Even this sexist comment sounds like a professional compliment.

"I am sorry if I got carried away. You see, there is a fairy tale among my people that if you ever do reach the end of a rainbow, a beautiful lass will be at the end. She will be yours forever and make love to you whenever you desire." He is salivating while his eyes keenly travel up and down my body.

"And so I came here, and you are here for me, all mine. So where do we begin? Let's see, let's see. Your garments must be uncomfortable to wear, and totally unnecessary on my land. Why not start with you taking off all of your clothes? It would give me an opportunity to examine a bit more closely your beautiful body that I will no doubt shortly be fornicating."

"We have a story, too, horny midget," I snap. "If you make it to the end of the rainbow and there is a pot of gold there, it is yours. This pot of gold is mine. Get lost before I kick you where it hurts." I do not like to be treated as property and am not his pot of gold.

I start walking away with my treasure and the little man starts crying. First peeps and then wailing. The further I walk away, the more he cries. I turn around and see him sitting on a large mushroom, his eyes hidden in his lap, and he continues to cry.

"Get lost," I yell back to him.

"I have been alone for so many years and this is the first time I have had a chance to have a conversation with a beautiful lady and she walks away. Oh, why me, why me?"

He continues to blubber. Maybe I could have been easier on him. I also like hearing the phrase "beautiful lady." So I put my cauldron down near my horse and walk back to him.

He looks up from his hands.

"I guess I can talk with you for a few minutes," I say reluctantly.

"Oh goodie, oh goodie, someone to talk with!" He jumps up and down with excitement. It is almost comical how quickly he went from crying to jubilation.

"Wonderful, wonderful. Here, sit next to me."

I sit down next to him on the large mushroom.

"Now what to talk about? What to talk about? Yes, I know, I know. Please start by telling me all about how you lost your virginity," he begins. "Please describe it in detail, including the position in which you were penetrated. I also would like to hear your first impressions of what it felt like to have a penis inside of you."

"You've got to be kidding me, you little pervert," I say in shock.

"I'm sorry, I don't know how to converse with someone so beautiful. Let me start again. Let's see...let's see...how did it feel when a boy first put their hands on that lovely tight tush of yours? Did it stir something inside of you? Did the lucky boy squeeze, grab, or pinch? What feelings did you experience? Please share."

These were real questions? I respond reactively, "I know it felt much better than it felt a minute ago when a little horny midget pinched me there."

"Not going well, not going well," he murmured. "Okay, what did it feel like the first time a boy put his tongue in your mouth? Were you expecting it? Did you lick his tongue back?"

"Strike three," I say and get up off the mushroom and start walking back toward my horse.

Then I hear the most beautiful music. I freeze in my tracks and turn back around to see that he is playing what looks like a small flute. Tears start streaming down my face. The song he is playing is so rich yet so sad. I walk back and sit next to him again while he plays, wiping tears on my arm. He finishes the song and then stops.

"I am so sorry, so sorry, young lass." He is starting to sob again. "I don't know how to talk to a pretty girl like you, especially one with such delicious lovely curves including a most juicy ass." He starts rubbing together the two fingers that pinched me. "Possibly the juiciest."

I stand up again, so he changes the subject. "Where are my manners? I apologize for not introducing myself. My name is Alfie, and I am what you might know as a leprechaun."

"The green, the rainbow, the pot of gold, your height, or lack thereof... I kind of knew you were one already."

"You are a kind and observant girl, I see. I live in these woods. You are on leprechaun land, and therefore I am your gracious host. Please, if my words offend you, join me for a few more songs and then be on your way. It would make me so happy for you to listen to me play."

I sit back down next to him, and he offers me his pipe. I pictured Siyo's ancestors using a pipe as a peace offering, and I guess Alfie is also trying to make peace.

"Thank you," I say and put the pipe in my mouth and puff. I start choking right away, and Alfie slaps me on the back. Actually because he is so short, he slaps me on my lower back, probably by most standards technically my bottom. Anything to get near my rear. At this point, I find myself going from choking to laughing and then he starts laughing too.

"This is strong stuff," I say.

"Nothing better," he says.

I continue to puff on the pipe, and Alfie continues to play his small flute.

Again, tears stream down my cheeks as he plays. It is the saddest most beautiful melody I have heard. It is an old Irish song in the style of *Danny Boy*.

He sees my tears and puts his hand on my knee and taps gently. "There, there, lovely lass." He keeps his hand on my jeans as the music continues.

The more I puff on the pipe, the more relaxed I become. There is definitely some good stuff in that pipe, probably illegal in most states.

I continue to listen to the music and look down at Alfie's hand on my knee. His hand is small and stubby with lots of bright red short curly hairs. His hand is a cross between a small boy's and an orangutan's.

He starts moving his hand in small circles on my knee. He continues to play from his flute, while I take another puff from the pipe and listen to his music. It is impressive that Alfie can play these beautiful songs with just one hand.

I am hovering between relaxation and hypnotism. His music seems to be in synch with the trees swaying. The pattern he is making on my knee becomes larger and encompasses almost my entire thigh as well. His other hand continues to hold his flute, and he is looking out into the distance, not even at me, playing, while his hand's movements or his music or the crazy shit in this pipe continues to pull me more and more into a trance.

When the circles reach the length of my whole thigh, he starts letting his small stubby pinky come into contact with the area between my legs. It does not seem to be purposeful, but whenever his stubby pinky finger rubs against my sex, it tickles and I shiver slightly.

He seems to slow down the speed of his circles when he approaches my sex, and not just his finger but his whole hand seems to be massaging that area. I spread my legs wider, making it easier for him to reach my crotch. Even through my jeans, I am getting aroused.

These hand movements introduce sensuality into the mix – I am feeling not only relaxed and dreamy, but also passionate. I close my eyes and enjoy the emotions and feelings and the music.

I snap out of my dream-like state at the sound of a zipper opening.

I open my eyes, and the leprechaun is on his knees before me, in between my legs, and he has unbuttoned my jeans and pulled down my zipper! His music has stopped and both hands are busy at work.

I put down the pipe and stand up to try to get back to my horse, and he uses the opportunity of me standing up to pull both my pants and panties down to my ankles. I try walking and trip, falling forward on the soft grass.

Alfie turns me over and puts his small mouth over mine, kissing me aggressively. I want to barf, but everything is happening in slow motion, I cannot imagine what barf would look like coming out of my mouth in slow motion.

Without wasting any time, he pulls down his little pants, and I see his tiny flute, more like a piccolo, a small but excited piccolo. I also notice his curly green pubic hair – he has green pubic hair! Gross!

He crawls in between my legs, pulls up my bikini top, and licks my breasts. My nipples react to his tongue action. "Oh, I am so excited about penetrating my lovely lass, and I can see you are too, my little naughty girl. Do you have a little Irish in you? If not, you are about to get some."

He pushes up into me, so his little piccolo is all the way inside me. "What a lovely body you have, and a perfect fit for me!"

He is too small to pump and lick my breasts at the same time. So he shimmies himself lower so he can push back and forth and grab my breasts for support. I feel his chubby little hands gripped tightly over my nipples. He starts pumping.

"Get off me, you creep," I say.

"Oh, my naughty lass. Look how excited your nipples are. And you are excited somewhere else, too, I can feel it. Just lay back and let Alfie do the work now. You have a lovely body and deserve to sit back and relax while it is fondled and violated." His face starts contorting slightly. "Yes, that's good, very good. Yes, yes!"

Where are my hands? Why can't I push this little creep away? I try reaching up but my hands feel like lead baseball bats. What makes me feel even worse is I know he is a skilled lover, as his movements have the same effects on my body as his flute playing did on my heart. He knows how to touch me, even if he is doing so against my will. There is rhythm to his pumping and groping.

I close my eyes and pretend I am with Siyo instead of this little midget. I smile. Alfie notices right away.

"Good, good, good. Almost done, at least for our first time together. I have so much built up for years, I can't wait to let it go. Oh, here it comes!"

He keeps the same movement while he is pulsing inside of me, and it becomes wet down there. He stops after several more thrusts and rests his head on my breasts.

"I am glad I listened to those fairy tales about what's at the end of the rainbow," he says slightly out of breath. "I know you want more right now, but we need to wait at least a few moments, my lovely lass. Please be patient. I will entertain you as we wait."

He raises his head from my breasts and moves up to my lips and starts kissing me again heavily, tongue to tongue. He has a small tongue, but even for a small tongue he is quickly able to locate my hiding tongue, pry it out, and lick it up and down. I want to be repulsed by this ugly tiny man, but instead I'm excited and find it all very arousing. With his lips tight against mine, he digs his nails brutishly into the soft skin on my backside.

He then turns me back over and licks my backside. It's very erotic. Even though I am focusing my thoughts on Siyo and the earthy smell of the grass that is right up in my face, I love the feeling this leprechaun is giving me.

"I knew I would get this lass' ass," he says, almost to a tune while he caresses my bottom. "What a prize. Now for round two, as all of this licking has increased my appetite. For this next position, I would like to keep my eyes on your tight tasty tush and see how it jiggles while I pound it hard during our next little mating routine. Hope you don't mind, lass."

I am about to tell him that I do mind and to stop calling me "lass," when I feel him inside of me again. He places his hands on my waist and pulls me toward him slightly, so he has the angle he wants for pumping.

His pumping action is the same. I feel him slap against my bottom with every pelvic push. I try to picture Siyo making love to me.

"That's it, lass. Your ass provides such a soft cushion for each bang, and it jiggles so delightfully after each thrust. I might use this position the next twenty or thirty times, and then afterwards if I tire, I will allow you to do some of the work. I would imagine it would be enjoyable to have you on top and for me to be charmed by your bouncing big boobs."

I feel his rhythm speeding up and know he will release soon. This is a nasty position and is purely just for his own enjoyment. I may still be in some sort of trance but I do have some strength. I am able to roll over on my side, and the leprechaun slips out of me onto the grass with a small thud.

I start laughing. Not just a giggle but uncontrollable laughter and even snorting.

"You think this is funny?" the leprechaun asks, obviously offended. "I am making love to you and you push me away. Do you know how rare it is to receive leprechaun love juice?"

I am about to make a comment back when he continues, "This lovely ass of yours is mine."

I continue to laugh at this whole situation. He continues, "Mine, like that pot of gold you tried to steal from me. I will give you one coin though. Consider it a souvenir."

He takes one gold coin out of his pocket and shows it to me. It turns bright red in his hands, molten hot. He then presses the coin mercilessly against my backside and I scream.

I screamed myself awake and heard my dad's voice. "Everything okay, Jennifer?"

I got myself together. "Yes, just a bad dream. Sorry about waking you." I could have said, *A zebra can't change their stripes and as hard as Siyo tries to be a good boyfriend, his dick gets in the way, along with his dark fantasies.* I don't think my dad would understand.

Chilled Watermelon Soup

I read about a study that revealed watermelon may have the same effects on our bodies as Viagra! Imagine the results of a Viagra-eating contest! I'll stick to a watermelon eating contest, thank you very much.

This chilled watermelon soup will take the edge of those steamy summer nights.

Scoop out enough of a seedless watermelon to fill your blender ¾ to the top. Then add any combination of lime juice, strawberries, dates, figs, or mint leaves. Throw in a handful of ice cubes and blend on high until everything is fully mixed.

Pour into cups and serve!

Caught

I stayed in bed staring at the ceiling, thinking about Siyo and his dream snatcher. I had decided to break up with Siyo, and this did not upset me. I knew though that Siyo would use that dream snatcher on his next girlfriend, and the one after that, and so on, and maybe the outcomes would be worse than simply breaking up with him. Maybe some of the girls he seduces through his dreams would have outcomes similar to what happened to

Siyo's grandmother. I shuddered at the thought of
Amy killing herself.

At the end of Spanish class, I approached Siyo.

"Can I stop by after school?"

"You were okay with that dream?" Siyo asked.

"I didn't like it as much as the ghost dream, but the
kinky themes are starting to grow on me."

"Would you like another one tonight?"

"Definitely. You can start increasing the volume on
the perversion scale, and I'll let you know when it
gets too much. Maybe we can both benefit from
these dreams. I can increase the naughtiness level I
can tolerate, and you can work on being more
romantic. Last night's dream helped build up my
endurance, especially after being screwed twice by
a leprechaun."

Siyo laughed and said, "Kind of proves that size
doesn't matter, huh?" I laughed too, the silly laugh
when I want to politely end a conversation.

"Let's meet at the flagpole and then we can walk home together. My parents are both working late tonight. Hint, hint."

I chuckled. "It's a date. I have to do a shift at the diner tonight, so wait for me five minutes at the flag pole, I have to change first."

Siyo nodded.

After my last class, I changed into my waitress uniform. As I approached the flag pole, I saw Siyo leaning against it, talking with Amy. I wondered if Siyo did this as payback for me taking Steve's phone number. I started to feel jealously boil slightly inside of me, but quickly turned it off. I needed to prevent Amy from being Siyo's next victim, so I quickened my pace toward the flag pole and pity replaced jealously.

Siyo saw me approaching and although I might have imagined it, I saw Siyo lean closer in toward Amy.

"Hi, guys," I said cheerfully.

"Hey," Siyo responded, with a tone that conveyed he got caught with his hand in the cookie jar. He turned away.

What a good actor. Amy looked happy to see me. "Hey, Jenn, working tonight?"

"Yeah, not a long shift though."

We chatted some more and then Siyo and I said bye to Amy and walked toward our homes.

As soon as we entered Siyo's house, I put down my school bag and pinned him against the door and gave him a big French kiss. He didn't resist, but after I released him, he asked, "Where did that come from?"

"I'll do anything so that you'll stay with me instead of date Amy."

I could see his arousal level increase. "I'll be right back." Siyo ran to his bedroom and in less than ten seconds returned with the snatcher and a Band-Aid. "You deserve a special dream tonight. Give me your hand."

I did not expect him to pass up real sex with dream sex, but reluctantly stretched out my hand. He reopened my paper cut, which had almost scabbed over. He quickly put a Band-Aid over it. "I'll be right back," he said and brought the dream snatcher back to his bedroom.

When he returned, I pleaded with him. "I can't stand to see you with Amy. You are breaking my heart." I took his hand and pressed it against my chest over my heart. "Do you feel my heart beating? You can tell I missed you, right? My heart has always belonged to you."

I kept his hand on my breast and took his other hand and placed it on my backside. I could tell his level of arousal had increased substantially, his shaft waiting anxiously to be free. It helped that I wore my waitress outfit with skintight spandex pants.

"I am now a skilled waitress, you know. I would like to take your order. What would you like? Or to be more precise, how would you like me?"

"Surprise me," he said, loving every second of this.

I gently removed his hands from my body, giving each hand a lick as I did and walked him toward his bedroom.

I laid him down in his bed. I noticed the dream snatcher on his dresser, near some other odd-looking Indian dust collectors.

I turned on the clock radio next to his bed and moved the radio tuner, looking for something to help with the mood. I quickly went through half the FM dial until I came to an eighties music station playing Billy Ocean's, "Get Outta My Dreams, Get Into My Car." Yes, this song seemed appropriate. I blasted the volume and started dancing.

I had no idea how a stripper dances, but I knew I could wing it. I started shaking everything I had to the music. I moved my head in circles and before the song finished I had taken off my vest, blouse, bra, and ponytail holder. I danced topless wildly over to him and let my hair hit him, waving my hair back and forth across in his face.

"You go, girl," he said and started to loosen his jeans.

I went back in front of the bed and started humping his bed post. This either looked over-the-top sexy or completely weird or maybe both, but I kept doing this wild dance.

Next, I ran my fingers back and forth in between the elastic of my spandex pants and my waist. Then I slowly bent over with my back to him and pulled my pants down, giving Siyo an unobstructed view of my bright white panties.

I pulled the pants over my feet and start spinning them wildly in the air, trying to keep in tempo with the music. I slowly approached Siyo, dancing alongside his dresser with one hand swinging my pants. I quickly reached out my other hand and grabbed the dream snatcher off his dresser!

Before Siyo could react, I ran into the bathroom in his bedroom with all of my clothes and locked the door.

Siyo banged on the door, "Hey, not funny. Open the door. Your show's not over yet." He obviously hadn't noticed that I grabbed his dream snatcher.

I flushed the toilet and I knew Siyo had realized what I did when he banged on the bathroom door and yelled the single word, "Bitch!"

I got dressed and then opened the door. He rushed past me to the toilet and stuck his hand in, not caring what contents might have been in that toilet recently. He stretched his hand in all the way and couldn't feel anything.

"You tricked me, didn't you? Flushed the dream snatcher so that I can't control any more of your dreams. Do you know how valuable that snatcher was? Just the silver content alone?"

"Siyo, it turns you into a bad boy. Without that snatcher, you could become a caring romantic boyfriend. Want to try?"

"Get lost, bitch."

He used that word again. I hated that word. In fact, I didn't like being here anymore.

"I don't want you back anyway. Amy is hotter, and I am going to call her as soon as you get your ass out of my house," he said as I walked toward the door.

He came to the door and kept yelling at me as I approached my car. "I am still the controller in one last dream. I planned to give you one I thought you might enjoy tonight. But this definitely changes things." He paused for a moment before continuing. "You did say your heart belongs to me."

As I walked the remaining distance to my house, I felt good about what I'd done. Even if he gave me an awful dream tonight, at least he could no longer be the controller for any girl's dreams.

Before leaving for work, I dropped my school bag off. I also went into my bedroom and pulled up my blouse and pulled down my pants. I gently reached my hand into the front of my panties and took out the dream snatcher, neatly wrapped with several layers of toilet paper to prevent getting cut from the sharp edges. I opened my nightstand drawer and gently slid it underneath some books. *Controller*, I liked that title.

After my shift, I felt beat. I had a late dinner with my parents and then showered and jumped under the covers. I took my Band-Aid off and examined my cut finger. I had hoped to steal the dream snatcher before Siyo cut me, but I guess I could take anything in a dream.

My shift at the diner is finally over, and I am walking to my car. It must be close to midnight, and it is a cool evening. There are no other cars in the parking lot, and I am parked in employee parking, about as far away from the diner as you can get.

As I get closer to my car, I realize how quiet it is. In fact, the only sounds I hear are the sounds of my heels against the pavement.

"You were naughty today." I stop in my tracks and spin around. Near one of the bushes alongside the restaurant is Siyo. He takes a step away from the bush and some of the light from the parking lot lights reveal his form. Siyo's face, but his body is a spider! A huge spider. He starts crawling toward me.

My car is not far away. If I run, I can probably make it.

"I could use a hug. Especially after your evil stunt today," Spider-Siyo continues. "Come here and give me a hug."

I ignore him and start walking toward my car. I have my keys out already.

"Give me a hug, and I'll leave you quickly and without too much harm."

I turn around. He is still far behind me, and I am close to my car. He stops crawling to make a hugging motion with his eight legs. I could not see myself being embraced like that, so I continue walking toward my car.

"Remember, you said your heart belongs to me. If you don't give it to me, I may need to take it from you."

I ignore this threat as I am just a few feet from my car.

Caught!

I walk into a spider web. Not a little spider web that you can brush away with your hands. I am caught in a giant spider web. I hate spider webs and to be actually stuck in one and not be able to brush it off feels even worse. I rapidly move my arms, legs and head, trying to get myself free, but the more I move, the more tangled I become. I can almost touch the door handle of my car. The invisible web caught me right in front of my car. I am stuck in a trap, a fly in Siyo's web.

I am several feet in the air, trying to spin free. The web is over my face, and although I can see, my mouth is completely covered so I cannot speak. I try to scream for help but nothing comes out. Maybe somebody driving by will see me, or maybe the busboys, who usually stay at the diner later than me to clean up, will come to my rescue. My hands and legs are spread apart wide in a jumping jack position. The more I move, the more tangled I get.

I stop moving and let myself be stuck. I now know what a fly feels like when it gives up in the web. I am a fly. I feel tired, tiny, and helpless.

I hear Siyo's evil laugh behind me, getting louder, so I know he is scurrying toward me. I cannot see him because I am facing the other way toward my car. At this point, I am too tangled to even spin around and face him.

It is a scary feeling to be completely helpless, caught in a web and at the mercy of your ex-boyfriend, who happens to be a sadistic spider.

His laughter stops, and I feel he is close to me. That makes me even more scared.

The web starts moving around me, as he is climbing closer. I feel him crawl up my legs and back. He is on me now, and I can completely sympathize with that poor fly. He is breathing on my neck, and I feel what must be his saliva dripping down my neck and back.

"You should not have run from me," Siyo says. "You are mine. Tell me you are mine and that your heart belongs to me. I can easily let you go, you know."

I could not speak if I wanted to. His web covered my mouth. "Nod your head," he continues, "to say that you are mine. Mine to do with as I wish."

I do not nod my head. If I could speak, I would tell him to fuck off.

I can tell he is angry.

"Then I take what I want, and I will punish you." And he spins me around so we are eye to eye. I try not to look at his spider body, and just keep eye contact with him.

He raises one of his eight legs, if you could call them legs, up to my face. The tip of his leg has a sharp black point at the end, which looks like a giant rose bush thorn. So sharp that its blackness shines like a knife under the parking lot light. He lets the furry part of his leg brush across my face, gently touching my cheek. My tears start falling. Maybe he will let me go now, I think stupidly. Siyo would not physically hurt me, would he?

His leg works its way down and gently rubs my breasts through my black vest and white blouse.

"Such beautiful breasts. I have held them and caressed them on more than one occasion. They are a work of art." And then he hesitates before adding, "What a pity."

He places the tip of the sharp point of his leg against my chest, pressing against my vest and blouse. He applies a small amount of pressure and the sharp point makes a hole through the thick vest and silky blouse. It hurts. I feel warm liquid drip from my breast and know I am bleeding. An evil grin appears on his face. He applies more pressure. By the pain I feel, I know his point has cut deeper into my skin. He continues to apply pressure. The sharp point works its way forward, into me.

I look down, and then quickly look up again, aware that I have been stabbed by something at least as sharp as a knife. I feel more warm liquid all over my chest. He is going to kill me.

I lock eyes with Siyo as he continues to apply pressure to his spider point. The pain is unbearable. I am afraid to glance down, as I know what I will see – my left breast sliced open and lots of blood. I don't like the sight of blood, especially when it is my own. I keep my eye contact with him and will not give him the satisfaction of screaming or appearing in pain. He grins with his spider fangs showing and keeps his eyes locked with mine as his leg continues to push forward, into my breast, deep into my body. I try to smile back to fake courage, and then realize that he can't see my smile anyway behind the web covering my mouth.

So this is what it is like to be stabbed and killed with a knife. What a way to go, killed by a giant spider with your ex-boyfriend's face.

While wondering how much further the sharp point can go before coming out my other side, I hear a whooshing sound and Siyo pulls out his leg from my body. There is something stuck on the sharp point on his leg, and under the parking lot light I see it is my heart. How can I still be alive if he is holding my heart? My heart is completely speared. He brings it up to his face and licks my bloody heart, and then licks around his lips. He is eyeing my heart with satisfaction written all over his face. I look at my heart, too. It is beautiful, still beating slightly.

"You did say your heart belongs to me, didn't you?" He lets out an angry laugh. "I am just taking what is rightfully mine."

He then pulls my heart off the sharp point and puts it up to his mouth. A thin silvery line of a spider web comes out. He starts turning my heart round and round, wrapping my heart up in his spider web, like running tape around a package. Very quickly, my heart is fully sealed in the silvery web, and he gently puts it on the ground next to him.

"I have my present. Now for your present." He takes out some more spider web from his mouth and constructs what looks like a whip. I know it is a whip because he moves it quickly in the air and it makes a snapping sound.

"A gift for you." He grins and spins me back around.

The whip makes contact with my backside. It stings, even through my spandex pants, but I hold back the pain and tears. He continues to whip. Again and again. I feel blood dripping down my legs. He is not stopping though.

"I don't need you anymore," he cries, out of breath. "I already have your heart."

I put the pain out of my mind, but flinch every time that whip hits what is left of my behind. He continues to rant, whipping me with all his might.

He is getting tired, I can feel it, as there is more time between whips and he is out of breath. "You...you will not be able to," another whip, "sit down again." One last whip followed by a shrill laugh.

He spins me back around so he can look in my eyes one last time.

"I am done...I am done and over you...goodbye." He bends over and picks up my heart. He slowly crawls away. There is nobody in the parking lot but me, and I am dangling, and bleeding, no heart, and all alone.

Sunlight woke me up. Light shone through my shades and it looked like it would be a beautiful Friday. The feelings of pain and loneliness from that dream were quickly replaced with a feeling of excitement that I have a date with Steve on Sunday.

Coffee with Cinnamon

I love coffee. Not decaf, but the real thing. I am not ashamed to say that I am addicted to coffee. Caffeine is not all bad though, and maybe even more good than bad. Caffeine is a stimulant and that means it speeds up the heart rate (think arousal!) and makes the blood flow.

This recipe is so simple, it is just one sentence. Place a sprinkle of cinnamon in the ground coffee and make coffee as you normally would. If you can't make coffee, go to your local coffee shop and add cinnamon instead of sugar. It is healthier for you and tastes out of this world!

Controller

The sun woke me Sunday morning, and I jumped out of bed, excited for the day.

I opened my bedroom door and inhaled the familiar breakfast smells and heard my parents talking. I joined them at the kitchen table. After my parents shared some work stories and me some school stories, I told them that I broke up with Siyo.

My parents looked at me, surprised. My dad said, "I'm sorry, honey."

"Don't be sorry, it went on for much longer than it should have."

"But you and Siyo looked so happy together," my mom said.

"We had fun most of the time, but I got to see a part of Siyo that made me realize he is not the one for me." I didn't tell my parents which part of Siyo. "Besides, I am going on a date today."

"With someone new?" my mom asked, sounding worried.

"Yes, I met him at the diner. His name is Steve."

"How did you meet Steve?" my father asked.

I told them and also that he lived in New York and went to college there.

"Don't trust anyone from New York," my dad said. "They tend to be a lot faster than boys from around these parts."

"I'll be careful." I then told them what we had planned for the date, and that Steve would be stopping by to pick me up so they could meet him.

I ran some errands with my parents and helped them do some cleaning around the house. They were worried about making a good first impression. I told them not to worry. Steve and I were going on a first date, he is not coming here to ask your permission to marry me. We all laughed.

I chose to wear jeans and a spring sweater. I definitely did not want to wear a dress, and there is no way we are playing Frog Bog. If I see a freaky-looking puppet at any of the boardwalk games, I will run in the opposite direction.

The doorbell rang exactly at three. I let my parents get the door, while I finished getting ready. This would give Steve a chance to talk with my parents. It would make my parents more comfortable with this stranger, I hoped.

When I came out about ten minutes later, Steve had been enjoying a bowl of ice cream and talking to my parents between spoonfuls. When he saw me, he stood up and stretched his hand out to shake my hand, but instead of shaking my hand he just held it for a long moment, smiling at me with that adorable smile. I blushed.

"I'm hoping ice cream won't ruin my appetite for dinner," Steve said. "But your parents offered me Mint Chocolate Chip, and I can never pass up Mint

Chocolate Chip. That is my favorite flavor." My parents seemed pleased.

"If you want more, Steve, let me know. Plenty more in the freezer," my mom said.

"I better not," Steve said as he finished his bowl of ice cream and walked over to the sink. He rinsed out his bowl and spoon and put both in the dishwasher.

I knew even by this first encounter that they liked Steve. I liked him, too.

"What year is your Jaguar?" my dad asked Steve.

"1996. I bought it recently at a garage sale. So far it is running well – it feels like you are driving while seated on a sofa. Would you like to see it?"

Steve walked out with my dad while I went back to my room to get some tip money for games on the boardwalk. When I went outside, my dad and Steve had the hood of the car open and were talking about the engine.

They continued talking about the car, but when Steve noticed me he ran to open the passenger door. I didn't remember the last time anyone had opened a door for me. I can get used to this.

My dad told us to have fun. I felt the excitement of a first date as we drove to the boardwalk.

The Seaside boardwalk smelled of funnel cake and wood. The wood planks on the boardwalk give off a carnival-type odor when the sun heats them. You could smell it more in the middle of the summer but I felt a whiff of it in the air today too. Summer is just around the corner.

"Frog Bog!" Steve cheered as we approached the game. "I am amazing at this game. Come on, I'll win you a big prize." Steve started walked toward the Frog Bog, and I quickly grabbed his hand and pulled him in a different direction. I didn't even bother looking to see if a creepy puppet hung as one of the prizes.

"Let's play the darts game instead. My treat." I didn't let go of his hand. I liked the way it felt. Steve's large hands gently enveloped mine.

We played a bunch of games and although we did not win any prizes, we had lots of fun.

Steve bought a large bag of zepole. We watched the vendor fry the dough in oil and then drown the golden brown balls in powdered sugar. I love zepole, but I had my fill after the third one. I knew I had powdered sugar all over my face. Steve laughed when he saw my face covered with white powder.

"Wipe it off, big guy," I said.

Steve took out a napkin from his pocket but then put it away. "I can't waste all of that powdered sugar." He then surprised me by kissing the powdered sugar off my nose, then cheeks, and finally lips. He gave me a very sweet long kiss on my lips, probably extra sweet because of the sugar.

"Yum," he said after that kiss. "Powdered sugar tastes better on your face than even on the zepole." The rest of our date consisted of laughing, eating, holding hands, and of course, more kissing.

He dropped me off at home after dinner, around nine. He didn't want to keep me out late because I had school the next day. We said goodbye and hugged each other, a nice warm bear hug. I knew at that moment that I wanted to see him again.

"I had fun today, Steve. When can we see each other again?" I asked him.

"Maybe next Sunday? I can drive back down here and we can get together."

"It's a date." I gave him one more kiss at the door.

Then I whispered, "But I also want to see you later tonight. Wait here one second." I went inside and a moment later returned with a large silver object and a Band-Aid.

"Give me your hand," I told Steve.

He stretched his hand out to me cautiously.

"Trust me."